'Your boat is ~~~~~~~~~~~~~~'

'I paid good ~~~~~~
continued acc ~~~~~~
is bigger than ~~~

'You own a boa ~~~~ was incredulous,
and his gaze wen ~~~ ner like a magnifying
glass over a particularly interesting insect.

Rose found her colour rising. Since she'd
taken over her grandfather's business, she'd
put any pretence at femininity aside. She
didn't have time to remember she was a
woman. This man, though. . . This man made
her feel every inch a woman, and she didn't
like it one bit!

Marion Lennox has had a variety of careers—medical receptionist, computer programmer and teacher. Married, with two young children, she now lives in rural Victoria, Australia. Her wish for an occupation which would allow her to remain at home with her children, her dog and the budgie, led her to attempt writing a novel, and she has now published several.

Recent titles by the same author:

STORM HAVEN
ONE CARING HEART
LEGACY OF SHADOWS
A LOVING LEGACY

PRACTICE MAKES MARRIAGE

BY

MARION LENNOX

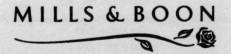

MILLS & BOON LIMITED
ETON HOUSE, 18–24 PARADISE ROAD
RICHMOND, SURREY, TW9 1SR

This book, and others before it, would not have been possible without the advice and encouragement of my friends, Philip and Leslie. Thank you both for your generosity, obstetric and gastronomic.

MILLS & BOON, the Rose Device and LOVE ON CALL are trademarks of the publisher.

First published in Great Britain 1995 by Mills & Boon Limited

© Marion Lennox 1995

Australian copyright 1995   Philippine copyright 1995 This edition 1995

ISBN 0 263 79034 7

Set in 10 on 10½ pt Linotron Times 03-9504-58305

Typeset in Great Britain by Centracet, Cambridge Made and printed in Great Britain

CHAPTER ONE

AFTER three hours and no crocodiles, Dr Rose O'Meara's tourists were hostile. They'd hired Rose to find a crocodile along the mud-flats, and nothing else would satisfy them.

Rose nosed her little boat up one branch of the river after another. As she searched she talked about life on the mangrove swamps. She pointed out mud-crabs, and cut her motor so her passengers could hear the bird-calls across the water. The high, sweet call of the oriole was worth the trip up the river on its own, she thought, and sometimes Rose decided it was almost worth the loss of her career. Almost. . .

And usually her tourists agreed with her. Not this lot, though. They only wanted a crocodile. Rose sighed as she rounded the last bend on the river. She'd be forced to offer their money back, and lose almost a week's profits.

But finally Big Bertha obliged. The huge crocodile lay half hidden by mangrove roots, sunning herself on the mud and looking for all the world like a harmless fallen tree-trunk. Rose steered her boat closer and her tourists were satisfied.

'Is it a man-eater?' a small child asked in delicious horror. He was the only passenger who had deemed this lady boat captain fun. 'Doc', the man on the wharf had called her as they boarded. It was a funny name for a crocodile hunter, but then she'd pulled a huge splinter from his leg and hadn't hurt at all. Maybe that was why they called her Doc.

She was pretty too, he decided, with her mass of red-brown hair and twinkly green eyes, despite the fact that she looked rather grubby. The child looked longingly at Rose's bare, brown legs. She looked much cooler than he was.

'She's a big one,' Rose said, responding to the small boy's need for a good shudder. 'If I were you I'd keep your toes tucked well inside the boat.'

'How can you tell if it's a man-eater?' an elderly lady demanded. She had been one of the most vocal in demanding her money's worth for the trip.

'Well, I guess the only sure way of knowing is by testing.' Rose said, forcing herself to smile. 'If I could have a volunteer. . .'

There was general laughter and the mood in the boat changed. By the time they were approaching the marina again, Rose's tourists were voting her trip worthwhile.

And so they should, Rose thought grimly. She'd taken them for an hour longer than usual and used much more fuel than she'd budgeted for.

She swung around the final bend in the river and thoughts of her budget were pushed aside. Her mooring at the marina was taken.

It was the last straw. Swearing silently, Rose pulled her little boat alongside the huge cabin cruiser and yelled upward. 'Hey! Is anyone there? You're in my mooring.'

There was no answer. The gleaming white and blue cruiser swung lazily on its mooring ropes, as if Rose's old, wooden *Crocalook* wasn't worth notice. For the first time Rose noticed a sign neatly painted in small letters on the cruiser's side. 'Marine Medical Centre'.

Medical Centre. . . Rose stared upward. What on earth. . .?

'Are you going to land us, or what?' Rose's obnoxious lady passenger demanded. 'We're an hour late already.'

There was nothing Rose could do. She stared helplessly up at the big boat and put the thought of the sign aside as too difficult to contemplate. For now she would be forced to unload her passengers at the bottom jetty, and they wouldn't like it one bit.

They didn't. By the time Rose had apologised sixteen times and refused point-blank to refund Miss Henry's money because Miss Henry hadn't bargained on walking half a mile, Rose's blood pressure was sky-high. She climbed up on to the jetty—the back jetty had no adjustable ramps—checked her mooring ropes, and stalked round to tell the owner of the cruiser exactly what she thought of him.

The boat blocking Rose's mooring was ten times as big as Rose's boat, and worth about a million dollars more. *Crocalook* wouldn't be worth what the owners of the cruiser had paid for their life-raft. The cruiser was streamlined and beautiful, painted a sparkling sea-blue with white trim, and with money screaming from every inch of its magnificent finish.

The cabin seemed bigger than Rose's house. It *was* bigger, Rose thought bitterly. It had enormous windows, smoked to prevent the nosy masses from seeing inside. Some medical centre! Rose thought bitterly. She glared at the windows for all she was worth and hoped someone was watching to take note of her anger.

A sign blocked the entrance to the jetty—Rose's jetty. 'Medical services available on board as of Monday,' it now proclaimed. 'Dr Ryan Connell. MB. BS. FRACP. Appointments advisable.' There was a telephone number and surgery times.

FRACP. . . Fellow of the Royal Australian College of Physicians. Not just a locum, then, it seemed. . .

'What the hell do they think they're playing at?' Rose demanded savagely of no one in particular. She lifted the sign aside and marched forward, on to the gleaming deck of the *Mandala*.

Rose had never been on such a boat before. Luxury cruisers occasionally pulled into Kora Bay, but their owners kept themselves very separate from the likes of Rose. Rose could see why. She looked longingly at the fittings on the deck. If she could afford ropes like this. . .and brass fittings. . . She shook her head. *Crocalook* was fitted out with an eye to economy. The owner of this boat had clearly never heard of the word.

The boat seemed deserted. Rose looked cautiously around. Surely a boat like this would have permanent crew. After moving the sign, Rose half expected security guards to swarm out and frog-march her off, and she was almost disappointed when they didn't appear. In her present mood she could have taken on a sumo wrestler or two.

Across the deck was a huge front door leading to the cabin beyond. Rose stared in awe. She'd never seen a door like that on a boat. Rose had never seen a door like that on a house. It was double-hinged, huge, and solid mahogany.

She wasn't going to be intimidated by any door. Rose raised her fist and banged hard, and then, too late, saw the gleaming gold bell with the elegant little sign telling her to push. To hell with it, she thought angrily, raised her fist and banged again.

'Unless it's an emergency we're not available until Monday. And if you break my door you'll pay for it.'

Rose jumped about a foot, her visions of sumo wrestlers still vivid, and wheeled to face the owner of the voice.

This man was no sumo wrestler. The man before her hadn't an ounce of spare flesh on his body. He was lean and he was angry. His anger almost matched Rose's.

'This is private property,' he said bluntly. 'Until Monday it's out of bounds. Unless it's an emergency then you telephone for an appointment.'

Rose took a moment to catch her breath. As she did she took in the man before her. He was older than Rose by ten years or more. She was twenty-six and he must be well into his thirties. His skin was tanned almost as deeply as hers, and his sun-bleached brown hair was tinged with premature grey. His smoke-

coloured eyes were creased against the harsh
Queensland sun, and they were dark with anger.

He was good-looking, Rose thought dispassionately;
at least, maybe he had been good-looking. At some
time in the not too distant past he'd had an argument
with something hot, and he hadn't come out of the
argument well. The left side of his face carried a
disfiguring burn scar, twisting his eyelid and making
him seem almost sinister. His left hand was likewise
scarred. Rose's eyes dropped to the twisted fingers. He
followed her gaze, made a harsh exclamation of dis-
gust, and thrust the hand deep into the pocket of his
tailored trousers.

'Would you like to tell me what you're doing here?'
he asked harshly.

'I came to tell you to get off my mooring.' Rose's
green eyes flashed anger at the man's near-black ones.
The sparks were almost visible. Rose drew herself up
to her full five feet five, wishing she could match his
extra six inches, dug her hands into the pockets of her
shorts and glared as hard as she was capable of glaring.

Amazingly, the anger being directed at her faded. It
was only a slight thaw, but the thaw was visible. Instead
of fury, the stranger's grey eyes showed the beginnings
of amusement.

'Your mooring,' he said blankly.

'Your boat is tied to my mooring,' she snapped. 'I
paid good money for this mooring. Just because your
boat is bigger than mine. . .'

'You own a boat?' His tone was incredulous.

'Of course I own a boat.'

His gaze went over her like a magnifying glass
over a particularly interesting insect. It took in her
taut, slim form, her bare brown legs and stained shorts,
her grubby T-shirt with 'O'Meara Croc Cruises' em-
blazoned across her breast, and her wild, chestnut curls
tied roughly back with a piece of black twine. Rose had
suffered engine trouble that morning, and it showed.

There was a long silence. The man's eyes rested on her, dropping to dwell with interest on her slim waist, where her shorts were hitched up with a worn leather belt. Rose found her colour rising. Since she'd taken over the boat she'd put any pretence at femininity aside. She didn't have time to remember she was a woman. This man, though. . . This man made her feel every inch a woman, and she didn't like it one bit.

'I own a boat,' she said again, her angry words cutting across the silence. 'And it's supposed to be moored right here. You have no right. . .'

'On the contrary,' he said smoothly. 'I have every right.' He lifted his good hand and retrieved a slip of paper from the pocket of his cream linen shirt. 'I have the rights to four moorings—all this end of the jetty, in fact. Kora Bay has no medical service, I gather, and the Marina Administration has agreed that I provide one. My mooring fees have been paid in advance.'

'But I've paid too. . .' Rose's astounded cry rang across the still waters of the estuary. A lone seagull lifted off his perch on the wharf and rose high against the late afternoon sun, as if looking for a better view of what was taking place on the cruiser.

The seagull was bound to be disappointed. Rose's words had been involuntary and even before she had uttered them she knew what had happened. The Marina Administration. . . She closed her eyes in disbelief. 'Roger!' she said savagely.

'I beg your pardon?' The stranger sounded bemused.

It had to be Roger. Rose's green eyes opened and flashed fury as she realised what must have happened. How dared he. . .? She took two angry steps towards the ramp leading from the deck back to the jetty, but the owner of the cruiser moved faster. He seized her shoulders and blocked her path.

'Let me go.' Rose pushed ineffectually against him, too angry to wait another moment. Roger Bain—the administrator of the marina—had set this up. He

wanted a medical service for his precious marina
because he thought the major tour operators wouldn't
bring tourists here until he had one. A medical service. . . Roger would do anything to achieve it. Rose's
teeth were almost grinding. 'Let me go,' she spat.

'If I release you, I risk you committing a murder.'
The stranger held her effortlessly in a grip of iron and
she was powerless to move.

'I risk doing a murder if I stay.' Rose's anger still
encompassed this man as well. If she had one tiny part
of the money the owner of this darned cruiser-cum-
medical centre so obviously possessed. . .

'Oh, really?' The man released her, but still stood
blocking her path to the jetty. 'Pistols at twenty paces,
or will you strangle me with your bare hands?' He
sounded amused.

'Let me go,' she snapped.

He shook his head and his eyes creased into a smile.
As they did the harsh, disfigured face transformed.
Rose stared up at him and came close to gasping. She'd
never seen. . .

What had she never seen? A man with the power
this man exuded? A man with a smile like this? She
stared up at him and her eyes were caught in his, like a
moth in a too powerful light.

With a shock she realised what she was doing and
she came down to earth with a jolt. She searched
desperately for her voice again. 'I'm trespassing on
your boat,' she said, and her voice wasn't quite steady.
'You don't want me here, and I no longer want to be
here. I'll get off now.'

'What's your name?'

'I don't. . .'

'If you want to get off you're going to have to tell me
your name.' He raised his twisted brow and crossed his
arms, standing directly in her path.

'It's no business. . .'

'You're on my boat,' he said pleasantly. 'On my boat we play by my rules. Your name?'

Rose took a deep breath, fighting for control of the situation and of herself. 'Rose O'Meara,' she said reluctantly.

He looked down at her T-shirt and his mouth twisted in a wry smile. 'Of course. I should have guessed.' He held out his right hand—his good hand. 'Dr Ryan Connell.'

Ryan Connell. Physician. Of course. Rose's mouth twisted in bitterness. 'I wish I could say I was happy to meet you,' Rose said through gritted teeth. 'But I'm not. Now, if you'll excuse me I have business to attend to.'

'Ah, yes. The murder.'

'I'm not going to murder anyone.'

'Promise?'

She stared up at him, surprised. His voice sounded almost serious. His eyes on her were intent and probing, and Rose felt her anger fade to be replaced by something undefined. Those eyes saw too much. They probed where they had no business probing. They made her feel. . .

She gave an impatient shrug, forcing her eyes away from his gaze. This man was an arrogant example of a rich medico and she was wasting time. It was Roger Bain who'd taken her mooring. She had to find Roger and find him fast.

'I promise,' she said harshly. 'Now can I go?'

He frowned and Rose had a fleeting impression that he was reluctant to release her. For a moment. . . For a moment she saw solitude behind his eyes, a solitude that was not in keeping with the man's hostility. Then she shook herself angrily. This man had his money and his precious medical service. And Rose. . . Rose had her mortgage, and if she didn't get this mess sorted out with Roger she'd end up another statistic in the bank's bad debt columns.

'You're going to see Roger Bain?' he asked.

'It's none of your business where I'm going.'

'Just answer my question.'

It was all Rose could do to stop herself giving him a mock salute. 'Yes, sir,' she said caustically. 'But I don't see. . .'

A yell brought her up short. From the far end of the jetty a man was waving wildly, running as he waved. 'Doc,' he yelled. 'Rose. . .'

Rose swivelled to stare down at the yelling figure. It was Leo Carter, a local fisherman. Leo was a man who never ran if he could walk and never walked if he could sit, but he was running now. 'Doc,' he yelled again. 'Can you come quick?'

Leo wouldn't yell like that if it wasn't an emergency. Rose was off the big cruiser and running swiftly along the jetty before Ryan Connell had time to think of stopping her.

Leo met her halfway along. He grabbed her arm, turned, and kept running, towing her after him. 'The kid,' he gasped. 'Rose. . . The kid. I only took my eyes off him for a second. Honest.' The big man was headed back to his mooring at a run.

'Lenny?' Lenny was Leo's four-year-old son.

'Yeah. . . I didn't see. . .' The words were coming in gasps while they ran. 'I. . . He's not breathing. He was only in the water for a minute. I. . . I didn't even hear him fall. . .'

Rose now knew as much as she needed to know. She put her head down and ran, and she reached Loe's boat before he did.

The child was sprawled limply on the deck of Leo's big fishing-boat. Beside him his mother was trying ineffectually to breathe into his lifeless mouth. Jenny Carter was sobbing too much to be any use at all and as Rose approached she raised a tearstained face.

'It's too late, Rose,' she moaned. 'He's. . . Oh, God, Rose, he's dead.'

Rose wasn't listening. In one swift movement she had jumped down on to the deck and had raised the child in her arms. Hanging him limply upside-down with one hand, with the other she searched in his mouth. A gush of sea-water came from Lenny's throat and Rose swiftly lowered him back on to the deck.

'Is he. . .? Oh, Rose. . .'

There was no time now for reassurance. Rose closed her mouth over the little boy's flaccid lips and breathed deeply. As she did she was aware of someone else beside her. A hand took Lenny's, and an increasingly familiar voice spoke urgently.

'No pulse. Keep on breathing and I'll take over CPR.'

Ryan Connell.

Strange how emotions could change so much in the period of minutes. Five minutes ago Rose had been appalled that a doctor had finally come to this sleepy little harbour. Now. . . Now she had never been more grateful for anything.

There was no time for reflection now, though. Rose put her head down and breathed solidly into the tiny face. Come on, Lenny, she whispered silently inside her head. Lenny was a spoilt but engaging urchin, who ran his parents ragged. He was their only child and if he was to die. . .

It didn't bear thinking of. Rose kept silently breathing. Above her she heard Ryan Connell snap questions as he rhythmically pummelled the tiny chest.

'How long was he in the water?'

'I. . . I don't know.' It was Leo. 'It can't have been more than two or three minutes.'

Ryan Connell's hands kept pumping, relentlessly moving the child's chest. His hands might be scarred but there was strength enough there for what he had to do. She breathed, and breathed again. Come on. Please. . .

And then Rose felt the tiny mouth quiver slightly

beneath hers. She might have been imagining it. Her breathing didn't falter, but she threw a questioning sideways look up at Ryan as she breathed. He lifted the limp hand once again, and his face cleared a little.

'Pulse,' he said softly. His hands eased their pumping. Rose breathed once more and then the small mouth moved definitely beneath hers. A rasping, choking breath. Another. Rose sat back as the child gagged, coughed, and started breathing for himself.

Oh, Lenny. Oh, baby. . .' Jenny Carter threw herself down on to the deck and gathered her child to her. 'Oh, my baby. . .'

'Keep him on his side,' Rose warned. 'I don't want him swallowing vomit. Leo, he'll still have water in his lungs. We need to get him to the marina first-aid room.'

'I've facilities on my boat,' Ryan Connell told her.

'But. . .'

'Does your first-aid room have X-ray equipment?' he demanded, and Rose shook her head.

'N. . . No.'

'Well, then.' He stood. 'Bring him straight down,' he ordered. 'I want to check those lungs.'

And suddenly Rose found herself redundant. Leo Carter gathered his dazed little boy into his arms and followed Ryan down on to the jetty. He cast an uncertain glance at Rose and she dredged up a smile.

'Dr Ryan will look after you,' she said softly.

'Rose. . . Rose, thank you. . .'

'There's no need for thanks,' Rose said. 'Just go. You don't need me any more. Dr Ryan's here.'

Rose stood watching them as they made their way swiftly across to the *Mandala*. Part of her was very close to tears.

She should be glad that Kora Bay finally had a doctor, she told herself harshly. She might have a medical degree but she wasn't qualified to practice medicine. It was only because she was Kora Bay's best approximation to a doctor that she had been called on in emergencies.

And now she wasn't needed any more.

'Grandpa still needs me,' she said sadly to herself, reminding herself harshly of the reason she had returned to Kora Bay in the first place. Her grandfather's need had never been enough to compensate for her loss of medicine, though.

'It has to be enough,' she said sharply. Crocodiles and her grandfather. That was her future. For however long it took. . .

There wasn't going to be any future if she didn't sort this mess out about the mooring. Rose took a deep breath, mentally girding herself for the fight to come. Roger Bain. . .

Roger Bain's office was on the second floor of the marina and Roger was in his office, as Rose had expected him to be. The man was always in his office. Rumour was that Roger had a socialite wife and two dreadful children at home, and Roger didn't like children. They wouldn't suit his style.

Roger's secretary stood as Rose burst into the reception area. She beamed a smile at Rose. 'How are you, Rose, dear?' she smiled. 'Have you heard the news?'

'That we have a doctor in town? I've heard,' Rose said grimly. 'He's in my mooring.'

'Yes, dear. We didn't have a choice, though.' The secretary spread her hands expressively.

'I want to see Roger.'

'I. . . I think he's busy. . .' the secretary faltered. 'If you'd like to take a seat. . .'

'I'll see if he's busy.' Rose brushed the secretary to one side and opened the door to Roger's inner sanctum.

Roger was standing, golf club in hand, aiming with care as Rose burst into the room. His vast office was carpeted in palest grey wool, with black leather furni-

ture elegantly placed. A practice putting-green had
been set up on one side of the office. It was almost the
same size as a real one.

Roger looked up for a fraction of a second as she
burst in, frowned, and then went back to his putting.
'Miss O'Meara, I'm busy,' he said curtly. Roger Bain
had never granted Rose her status as doctor. 'If you
want to see me, then make an appointment with my
secretary.'

Roger's secretary had followed Rose into the room,
bleating helplessly, 'I'm sorry, Mr Bain. I told
Rose. . .' She laid a hand tentatively on Rose's arm.
'You'll have to go, dear.' She looked helplessly over at
her boss.

Rose shrugged the woman off and stayed where she
was. She folded her arms and planted her bare feet
deeper into the soft wool carpet.

'I hope those feet aren't as dirty as they look,' Roger
Bain said smoothly, as if guessing her thoughts. 'If
you're staining my carpet, I'll bill you for the cleaning
costs.' The golf ball was struck cleanly. It ran forward
into the cup as though magnetised. Roger gave a
satisfied smirk, ran his hand across his slicked-down
hair and straightened. For the first time he really
looked at Rose, and what he saw made him grimace
even more. 'Miss O'Meara, you're hardly dressed
for. . .'

'I'm dressed for work,' Rose snapped. 'Which is
what I'm trying to do.' She reached into the pocket of
her shorts and retrieved a slip of paper. 'This is a
receipt, Roger. This receipt says I've paid for number
four berth on jetty two for the next month. What the
hell is going on?'

Roger sighed. 'You have been moved,' he said, as
though explaining something to a particularly stupid
child. He walked across to his desk, sat down in his
deep leather chair with his back to the view of the
estuary, and surveyed Rose with boredom. 'I believe

you've been reallocated to the back jetty. Isn't that right, Miss Graham?'

Miss Graham nodded furiously. 'It is, dear,' she told Rose. 'I pencilled you in. . .'

'I can't work from the back jetty and you know it,' Rose interjected. 'It's too far from the main wharf and it hasn't ramps or steps. My tourists can't clamber up a four-foot jetty wall. . .'

'It's only two feet at high tide,' Miss Graham broke in, but once again she was ignored. Rose stalked across and put her hands flat on to Roger's desk.

'You can't do this,' she said harshly. She shook her receipt at the man before her. 'My receipt says the mooring's mine.'

Roger leaned forward and flicked the piece of paper from her hand. He turned it over. '"If for any reason the given mooring becomes unusable",' he read, '"the administrator of the marina reserves the right to reallocate."' He handed the receipt back to her. 'See for yourself. You've been reallocated.'

'But it's not unusable. . .'

'It is,' Roger said smoothly. 'We intend to take up the boarding-ramp from number four mooring tomorrow for repainting. Dr Connell has sufficient access to his vessel from the boarding-ramps of moorings two and three.'

Rose's hands were clenched into fists. Her nails were digging into her palms so tightly that later she'd find she had made her palms bleed. There was no way of fighting this, and she knew it. She stared at the immaculately suited administrator before her while he watched her with bored eyes, and she knew she was finished.

'You know this will ruin me,' she said tightly. To her chagrin she felt hot, stinging tears well behind her eyes. 'I'm running on a shoestring now. Tourists aren't going to walk over to the back jetty. My main advertisement is my boat, and they won't even see it on the back jetty.'

'Miss O'Meara, I'm trying to build Kora Bay into a tourist destination. I can't do that without a quali- fied. . .' he dwelt lovingly on the word '. . .medical practitioner. Dr Connell's offer of a trial medical service is the answer to all my requirements and I'm not prepared to sacrifice it because your tourists don't like walking.' Roger smiled confidingly. 'And, frankly, there are enough tin-pot tourist operators working around these parts for your operation not to be missed, wouldn't you say, Miss O'Meara?' His smile broad- ened. 'The owners of the marina run a quite magnifi- cent crocodile-watching tour. . .'

'For ten times what I charge. . .'

'People pay for quality,' Roger said smoothly. 'As they'll pay for Dr Connell's services. They haven't been content with first aid from a half-trained doctor who doubles as a crocodile guide.'

'I'm fully qualified.'

'Then why aren't you registered?' He sighed. 'Now, if you've quite finished. . .' He looked across at his secretary. 'Show Miss O'Meara out, please, Miss Graham.'

Miss Graham looked helplessly over at Rose. 'You'll have to go, Rose,' she said.

'Why does she have to go?'

The cool, clipped voice came from the open door and involuntarily all three occupants of the room turned. Dr Ryan Connell was leaning against the door, calmly watching.

Roger Bain rose to his feet and came forward swiftly, his bored expression making way for one of beaming affability. 'Dr Connell,' he said smoothly. 'How are you? Settled in all right?'

'No.' Ryan Connell cast a glance at Rose's flushed face and overbright eyes and looked away. 'I thought you said I'd not be disturbed until Monday,' he said to the administrator. 'I've had one trespasser already, plus one medical emergency.'

Roger cast a look of venomous dislike at Rose. 'I can imagine,' he said disdainfully. 'Miss O'Meara, unless you would like me to call security I suggest you leave. I'd remind you also that you are still on call. You are required to provide emergency medical services until Monday, but no longer. And if I find you've been annoying Dr Connell I'll revoke your rights to the back jetty.'

'Are you a doctor?' Ryan Connell demanded, his brows snapping together.

'Miss O'Meara has some medical training, but is not a registered doctor,' Roger answered for her.

Rose bit her lip. There was no arguing with the administrator's statement. She turned back to Roger. 'You might as well take my mooring rights. The back jetty is useless and you know it.' She wiped her hand angrily across her face to remove an errant tear, leaving an oily smudge on her flushed cheek in the process. Damn them both. Damn Dr Ryan Connell and his money. Damn them. . . She stalked over to the door to leave with as much dignity as her bare feet and grubby shorts permitted.

'Wait.' It was a curt order. Ryan Connell put out a hand and stopped her. He held her loosely but she couldn't go past. Before she knew what he was about, he had lifted Rose's receipt from her nerveless fingers and was holding it up for closer inspection.

'That's mine,' she snapped, but he shook his head and kept reading, his good hand holding her idly at arm's length while his twisted hand held the paper.

'Just a moment,' he ordered curtly. He looked across at Roger. 'This says the lady's entitled to moor her boat on my jetty.'

'Of course she's not.' Roger Bain's urbane smile had slipped. 'Miss O'Meara was simply under a misapprehension. . .'

'I share that misapprehension.' The room was suddenly very still. Ryan Connell's voice cut through like a whip. 'Tell me why she has a receipt for the jetty where I'm moored.'

Roger shook his head. 'Dr Connell, we've supplied you with four berths and Miss O'Meara here is struggling to pay for one. I fail to see. . .'

'But Miss O'Meara paid first?'

Roger looked from Ryan Connell's cold grey eyes across to Rose and back again. He was clearly at a loss. 'Yes,' he finally admitted. 'But I don't see. . .'

'Then the berth is rightly Miss O'Meara's.' Ryan Connell was still fingering Rose's receipt.

'But you wanted the whole jetty.'

'I did,' the cruise boat owner admitted. 'I still do. But I'm not prepared to have this woman. . .' his eyes rested fleetingly on Rose as if he was unsure whether he'd used the right adjective '. . .removed from a position that's rightfully hers.' He shrugged. 'I can move the *Mandala* so it's not blocking mooring four. Move your boat back, Miss O'Meara.'

Rose was almost too stunned to respond. 'Th. . . Thank you,' she managed.

'I wish I could say it was my pleasure,' he said coldly. 'It isn't. There will be room at the end of the jetty for your disreputable craft, however. Just try to keep your activities from infringing on mine.'

Rose's fading anger rose again. The mooring was hers, legally and morally. She didn't have to show too much gratitude at receiving what she'd paid for and had every right to. She took a deep breath.

'I'll do my best,' she said icily. 'As long as you keep yours from infringing on mine.'

CHAPTER TWO

IT WAS dusk before Rose finally arrived home. She had called in to check on Rebecca Donovan's asthma, bought mud-crabs for her grandfather's dinner, and kept an appointment with the bank manager for another of her hated visits.

By the time she trudged up the overgrown path to her cottage she was exhausted. An errant bougainvillaea vine trailed down over the porch in crimson splendour. Rose pushed it back as she tried to balance key and groceries. The vine bit into her hand with a stinging barb and Rose winced. In this tropical climate, the bougainvillaea grew inches in a day. She'd have to find time soon to cut this vine back.

'Soon,' she muttered to herself. Soon was her most hated word. Soon she'd put the boat up on slips, repaint the woodwork and overhaul her sadly neglected engine. Soon she'd spend more time with her textbooks and journals. She was losing touch with her medicine. Soon she'd get the garden under control. Soon she'd pay off enough of her bank loan to cut her cruises down to once a day and spend more time with her medical books and with Pa.

'If I were Dr Ryan Connell I'd just hire servants,' she said bitterly, the thought of his arrogance and power making her shove the key into the lock with unnecessary force. For some reason just the thought of him made an angry flush come to her cheeks.

Why? The question came unbidden, and she tried to consider fairly. He had done the right thing by her. Despite Roger Bain she was still in business, thanks to Ryan Connell.

The thought gave her no pleasure at all. To be

beholden to such a man. . . And to have him practise medicine where she was forced to watch—to have the pain of losing the work she loved thrust under her nose every time she went near her boat. . .

If only it could be her. If only she could put her sign up on a surgery door and proclaim to the world she was Dr Rose O'Meara.

It was an empty dream, made even more remote now with the arrival of Dr Connell. She might as well stop even thinking about it.

The cottage was quiet as she entered and Rose frowned, the silence piercing her depression. Usually the wireless was on with the evening news when she arrived home. Rose frowned. 'Grandpa,' she called. 'Pa? I've bought mud-crabs.' There was no answer. The house was deathly still.

Thoughts of Ryan Connell and her abandoned medicine were shoved aside as Rose's mind filled with sudden panic. Pa should be here. He should. . . She dumped her groceries on the kitchen table and ran through the house. 'Pa?' The silence went on and on. 'Pa?' She was screaming his name, and in her voice was a sudden, dreadful knowledge. She knew. . . She reached the door through to the back veranda, swung it wide and stopped as her dread became reality.

The old man was dead. Slumped in his battered wicker chair, his old eyes staring sightlessly out across the estuary to the sea beyond, Rose's grandfather had slipped from life as quietly as he had lived. Rose didn't need her medical degree to know that he was dead. He had been dead for hours.

The world stopped. Rose's world hung crazily in limbo for one endless, timeless moment, and when it turned again her life had changed. Her world had tilted to a different angle and she felt as if she no longer knew the ground.

Slowly Rose crossed the veranda and knelt before her grandfather, taking the withered old hands in hers.

Gently she placed them under the blanket he had lying on his knees. She closed his eyes and then let her head fall against the rough fabric of his shirt. Sorrow washed over her in a cold and leaden wave.

She couldn't have asked for a better death for her grandfather than this, seated in the sun in his favourite chair, gazing out over the estuary that had been his home since he was a boy. He had been ill for so long. She wouldn't have wished him to live longer, but she would miss him so. . . Oh, Pa. . .

'Goodbye, Pa,' she whispered softly, and her words carried across the soft evening breeze and melted into the echoes of waves crashing on the distant shore. She kissed him gently on his leathery cheek and then she wept.

A long time later Rose rose stiffly to her feet, her mind blank and empty. Now what? She had never felt so unutterably alone.

Rose's parents had died when she was tiny. All her childhood there had just been Rose and Pa, and it had stayed like that until the old man had insisted she accept her scholarship for university. Tearfully Rose had left, travelling four hundred miles away to medical school.

After six years she had grown accustomed to a different life, forced to accept her grandfather's decree that there wasn't a future in O'Meara cruises and learning instead to love the medicine she was training for. Then the doctor visiting Kora Bay had written to Rose, spelling out how ill the old man was. Rose had just passed her last exam and had a year's residency to go before qualifying. The residency had had to wait. Pa had needed her.

'What the hell are you doing back?' her grandfather had demanded. 'Put me in a home, girl. Sell the boat and get the hell out of here.'

Some things just weren't possible. Rose's year of

residency had to be done in a teaching hospital and the nearest one was three hundred miles away. As well as that, residency meant twelve-hour working days or longer, and Pa needed Rose now as Rose had needed her grandfather in her childhood.

So Rose didn't make it as a doctor. Without her residency she couldn't practice. The marina officials employed her part-time as Kora Bay's first-aid officer. The locals called her Doc, because of her degree, but they all knew she wasn't fully qualified.

There was still *Crocalook*. Rose had found when she first came home that she could settle her grandfather happily in the bow of the boat while she ran the cruises. It had only been in the last few weeks that he had grown so weak he had wanted to stay at home.

She had been back at Kora Bay for two years now, and it hadn't been easy. In the years she had been away the marina had been built, and Rose's grandfather had been savagely billed for mooring fees. Rose had been stunned at just how far in debt her grandfather was—a year of mooring fees and no income because he'd been too ill to run the boat had just about ruined him.

'Sell the boat,' her grandfather had growled over and over again, but the boat had been their only source of income if Rose was to stay in Kora Bay. She must. Pa was Rose's best friend, and all the family she had. She had ignored the old man's protests, made him as comfortable as she could and proceeded to try and recoup the family fortunes. Two years later she was still at the edge of bankruptcy.

And now the old man was dead. The burden which had been hanging over Rose for the past two years slipped from her shoulders and she felt no joy in the knowledge at all. All that was left was emptiness.

'I can sell the boat and the house,' she whispered into the stillness. 'I can be out of debt.'

And then? Her future stretched bleakly out before

her. Residency back in the city. Medicine at last. There was no joy now in the prospect. She felt suddenly too old and too tired. She was a million years older than the student she had been two years ago.

I'll have to go, she thought bleakly. There's nothing here for me. And even if I do my residency I can't come back. Not if Dr Connell's here to stay.

She phoned Steve Prost, the doctor in the neighbouring town, and told him what had happened.

'Go ahead with the funeral arrangements,' Steve told her. 'I don't need to see him.'

Rose nodded bitterly as she made the arrangements for the undertaker to come for her grandfather. Steve had been leaving more and more of Kora Bay's medicine to her over the past few months, even to the point of countersigning prescriptions on his weekly visits. And she would miss the clinic at the marina.

'I'll have to sell the boat,' she whispered to herself, staring sadly out to the estuary as she put down the phone. 'I'll have to go.'

She was saying goodbye to both her grandfather and the life she had always known. Her childhood.

'It's all he's left me,' she said softly to herself. 'But it's a legacy that'll stay with me for the rest of my life.'

Unbidden, the thought of the new doctor on the expensively fitted cruiser came into mind. She remembered her impression of the man's solitude as she had walked off his boat. The man was alone, wealthy and aloof.

'See, Pa,' she said into the stillness, as though reassuring the old man. 'You might have left me heaps of money but still no happiness.' She looked down at her grubby toes and gave a rueful half-smile. 'What you've left. . .is me.'

Rose slept badly in the empty house, her sorrow gnawing at her even in sleep. She rose early and showered, then went out on the veranda to watch the dawn.

It seemed wrong to go to work today—to run O'Meara Cruises as if nothing had happened—but Rose couldn't afford the luxury of a day off. Not if the business was to survive. And if the cruises folded now she'd have no hope of selling it as a going concern.

'It'll be easier now,' she told herself sadly. She'd been paying a nurse to come in and spend some time with Pa during the day, and the costs of that plus Pa's medication had been crippling. Once the next mortgage payment was made it should ease, but there was that payment—plus the cost of the funeral. . . How much could she expect for the enterprise even if it was still running? Enough to cover the debt on the house?

She'd take the next day off for the funeral, she decided, but today she'd work as usual. Besides, there seemed nothing else to do. She had tourists booked for the morning cruise starting at eight. She glanced at her watch almost impatiently, eager to be out of the little house and away from her memories.

Despite her impatience, she was late for work. At seven-thirty the funeral home called with a list of arrangements that needed to be made for the following day. Rose battled through the list as well as she could, growing more and more upset, and then bicycled too fast down to the marina. She arrived flushed, emotional, and fifteen minutes late.

She'd moved her boat back where it belonged the night before, and her tourists had to pass Ryan Connell's cruiser to reach *Crocalook*. As Rose chained her bike to the rail at the edge of the marina she could see down on to the jetty and her heart sank. Ryan Connell was standing on the gleaming, wooden deck of the *Mandala* and he was clearly furious. There was a stream of tourists who'd obviously decided to check out the *Mandala* while they waited.

She wasn't ready for this sort of confrontation. Not

this morning. Still. . .there was no escaping it. She sighed and walked swiftly down on to the jetty.

'Well, well. . .' Ryan's icy anger reached her before Rose even reached the side of the *Mandala*. 'You've finally decided to show.'

Ryan Connell's anger was matched by the group of tourists on the jetty. One of them, a florid, overweight gentleman with a watch the size of a dinner plate and a clear blood pressure problem, stepped forward and thrust the watch under her nose.

'This cruise is twenty minutes late already,' he snapped. 'The wife and I are booked on a shopping tour this afternoon. We haven't time to waste. If we're late back. . .'

'I'm sorry,' Rose said placatingly. 'I. . . It was unavoidable.'

'There are other cruises, you know,' the man said harshly. 'The marina crocodile tour left ten minutes ago.'

'I'm sorry,' Rose repeated. She was past defending herself. 'If you'd like to board now. . .'

'Will we be back by twelve-thirty?'

'Yes,' Rose assured him.

The man gave an angry snort. 'I suppose that means we get a shorter trip,' he barked. 'I want my money's worth. . .'

'Shall we go?' Rose pleaded helplessly. 'If we don't get moving we'll be later still.' She stood at the head of the ramp and assisted her passengers down. It was as much as she could do not to burst into tears and run.

With the last of the passengers seated, Rose walked forward on the jetty to release the front mooring-rope. All the time Ryan Connell had been watching from the *Mandala's* deck, his anger palpable.

'I'd like an assurance that this won't happen again,' he said coldly. 'Your passengers seem to think my boat is a tourist attraction in its own right. Roy—my secretary—has better things to do than to stand guard. If they come on board again. . .'

'I said I'm sorry,' Rose snapped, fighting a losing battle with tears. 'Look, it's been one hell of a morning, Dr Connell. Can you just get off my back and leave me to my job?'

'Your job was to run this cruise at eight this morning. . .'

'Yes,' she said bitterly. She stared up at the man on his gleaming deck and something inside her snapped. The emotion and anger of the last twenty-four hours rose and washed over her in a cold rage. 'I was late. But I was late because I had things to do—urgent business to attend—which is more than can be said for you, Dr Ryan Connell. Do you know what work is? You stand there in your million-dollar cruiser and criticise me. . . And come Monday you'll start doing the work I've been squeezing into my off-duty time, and you'll charge like a wounded bull for it, and you'll complain how hard you're working. . .' She gave an angry gasp and choked back her mounting hysteria. 'As I said—I'm sorry,' she forced herself to say. 'It won't happen again.' She climbed down on to the deck of the *Crocalook* and turned her back decisively on the man above her. The sooner she got out of here the better.

Unfortunately *Crocalook* didn't agree. Rose turned the ignition key and the engine spluttered once and died. She turned it again and the same thing happened.

Damn. . . The word remained unsaid, but it went through and through Rose's mind. She had to overhaul this engine soon. There was that word again. Soon. . .

From behind there was an ominous silence. Her tourists were clearly tense and waiting. Rose turned the key and tried again with the same results. Nothing. Finally she bent forward and lifted the engine cover. As if on cue, her action released a tirade from behind her.

'What the hell. . .?'

'We're half an hour late already. . .'

'I told you we should have paid more for the professional tour. . .'

Rose bit her lip as her colour mounted. 'I'll have it going in a moment, ladies and gentlemen,' she promised. 'If you'll just be patient. . .'

'What seems to be the trouble?'

It was Ryan Connell's voice, cutting through the babble of protest with incisive calm. Rose looked up and her flushed face grew hotter. Ryan had come off the *Mandala* and was standing on the jetty, idly watching.

'It'll just be the points,' she said savagely.

'Do you know where the points are?'

Rose gave an angry gasp and looked back down into the engine, trying desperately to ignore him. Make yourself concentrate, she said to herself. Ignore him. If you get rattled. . .

She lifted each point in turn and scraped it clean with a screwdriver. She needed a rag. She looked around the boat and saw nothing that would do. Shrugging, she took the edge of her T-shirt and wiped across the contacts.

'Charming!' Ryan said coolly. 'No wonder you look such a grub.'

Rose's tourists had fallen silent. Ryan Connell obviously had them interested. Besides, there was no need to attack Rose when Ryan Connell was doing a fine job of it for them. They watched Rose's reaction with interest. The girl looked as though she would like to throw the screwdriver straight at Ryan Connell's head.

She didn't. Somehow Rose prevented herself. She re-attached her points, took a deep breath, and turned the ignition key. The motor purred into life. Rose sighed with relief while around her the tourists reacted

with near disappointment. They had lost a perfectly
good reason to complain.

Rose walked to the rear of the boat to remove the
stern mooring-rope but Ryan Connell was before her.
He unfastened the heavy rope from the bollard on the
jetty and lightly leapt down into the boat, coiling the
rope as he did.

'Thank you,' Rose said, trying to keep annoyance
from her voice. The man was trying to be helpful but
the boat was now drifting out. She'd have to return to
get Ryan Connell back on to the jetty.

'How much is your tour?' Ryan asked curtly, seeing
her frown.

'I'm booked out.'

He raised his eyebrows. 'Really, Miss O'Meara?'
Above the cabin a licence plate was screwed into
prominence. '"Licensed for seventeen passengers",' he
read aloud. He turned and did a swift head-count.
'There are fourteen, plus you,' he said calmly. 'How
does that make you booked out?'

'I don't. . .'

'You don't need another paying passenger?' he
asked. He smiled wryly. 'Fine. Consider me crew.' He
sank down on to the seat next to where Rose stood at
the tiller and folded his arms as if he had every
intention of staying. 'I'm here in case you need someone to push.'

Rose couldn't suppress an answering smile. The
thought of someone pushing a boat in these crocodile-
infested waters—especially if that man was Ryan
Connell—was almost appealing. As her sense of
humour reasserted itself she sighed and accepted the
inevitable. Ryan Connell was the last person she
wanted to take on her cruise but it looked as if she was
stuck with him. To manoeuvre the boat back to the
jetty now and force him to get off. . .

'OK, you can stay,' she said ungraciously. Then she

turned to her tourists. 'And you heard the man, ladies and gentlemen. He did promise to push. . .'

For the first hour or so, Rose's guided tour went well. The presence of Ryan seemed to calm the aggression in her tourists. Once they had left the jetty they appeared to settle back and enjoy Rose's patter. It was a superb morning, with the warm sun sparkling on the still waters of the river. It was almost low tide, and the roots of the mangroves were high out of the water, like weird, mud-coated sculptures.

Rose enjoyed her morning cruises more than the afternoon. The water came alive with the sounds of the birds nesting in the mangroves. The water was still and deep, and the little boat cut a white swath across its mirror-like surface. Once they were away from the marina they had the world to themselves. Every time Rose made the trip it refreshed and renewed her. Even this morning. . . Even with her grandfather's death and the presence of Ryan Connell beside her. Even now she could block out her problems, let her voice do its standard guided tour and her heart absorb the beauty and tranquillity of this place she loved so much. . .

But once again there wasn't a crocodile. They were an hour out before the tourists started getting restless, and Rose had to bring her attention solidly back to crocodile-searching.

Where were the darn things? She'd passed mud-banks where there were always crocodiles, only to find them empty. She frowned. It was only October. She should still be able to find one or two.

The crocodiles clearly had other ideas. The mud-banks stayed defiantly empty. Often the crocodiles were brilliantly camouflaged as logs, but the logs that lay there today were just that—logs. Even Big Bertha refused to co-operate this morning. Rose served her pre-prepared soft drinks and savouries to her passengers, ignored the silent Ryan Connell, and kept on searching.

'Time's getting on.' It was the man who'd made such a fuss on the jetty, staring pointedly at his over-sized watch. 'When did you say we'd be back?'

'We'll be back by twelve,' Rose said tightly.

'It's after eleven now,' the man said morosely.

'Sometimes the crocodiles just aren't here to be found,' Rose told him. 'My brochure says we try. . .'

'You advertise as croc-spotting,' the man said aggressively. He pulled himself up like a puff-toad at full excitement. 'I know my rights. No croc then no money. If you don't find a crocodile then we'll have our money back, thank you very much.'

Rose's heart sank. This group were from the same round-Australia tour as the people she had taken the day before. Clearly they had been practising their legal rights all around the country.

'I'm doing my best,' she said tightly. She cast a glance at Ryan Connell. He was leaning back watching her, his eyes expressionless. It was almost as if he was judging her, she thought, and she felt her colour mounting.

'Your best isn't good enough, girl,' the man snapped. 'Find us a crocodile, or else. . .'

'There's another one.'

The overweight tourist stopped mid-tirade. It was Ryan Connell who had spoken, for the first time since they had left the marina behind. Now Ryan was watching the mud-banks at the shoreline, his expression bored and uninterested. 'I don't know what the fuss is about,' he said lazily. 'While you've been talking I've spotted three.'

'Three. . .' Rose stared down at Ryan in astonishment. She was very good at spotting crocodiles. It was inconceivable that she'd missed three.

'Three,' he said decisively. 'There might have been more but I wasn't paying much attention.' He motioned

over to the bank and waved a bored hand. 'That one's
a big one. Male, I imagine. If you look hard you can
see a female over at the base of the dead mangrove
behind him. She's a bit harder to pick. Looks just like
a log. . .'

'Where. . .?' Rose couldn't see a thing.

Ryan frowned. 'Can't you even see the male? Really,
Miss O'Meara! Take the boat in closer.'

Rose obliged, her eyes searching the shore. All she
could see on the bank was a large, decomposing log,
sinking into the mud. With the tide so low she couldn't
get close enough to see it clearly, but she knew a log
when she saw one.

'I can't imagine how you missed it,' Ryan said
wearily. He smiled across at the puzzled tourists. 'It
seems we have a guide who can be fooled almost as
much as city folk.'

'I don't see any crocodile.' It was the man who'd
been berating Rose, and his voice was belligerent.

'Neither do I,' Rose agreed.

Ryan raised supercilious eyes at the rest of the boat.
'Two fooled,' he smiled. 'He's doing a great job, that
old man croc—just lying there, letting everyone think
he's a log. You need good eyes to pick him. If you look
really closely you can see the mounds of his eyes.
You'd think they were closed from here, but they're
watching all the same.'

'It's a log,' Rose snapped.

'Really?' Ryan gave her an incredulous nod. 'Can't
bear to be proved wrong, eh, Miss O'Meara? Let's see
you put it to the test, then. How about jumping out,
going over and giving your "log" a poke?'

Rose drew in her breath. To climb out of the boat
here was crazy. 'Don't be stupid,' she said harshly.

Ryan smiled around at the tourists. 'Well, well,' he
said softly. 'Point made. Are there any folk here with
eyes good enough to pick him from the log he's
pretending to be?'

It seemed there were. 'He just moved,' an old lady said triumphantly. 'I don't have city eyes. My sight's a hundred percent. My, isn't he huge!'

'I can see the female!' someone squeaked from the back of the boat, not wishing to be outdone. 'I think. . . I think she's got a nest back there. . .'

The aggressive male tourist looked from Rose's angry face across to the bank and back again. His mouth twisted into a triumphant smile. 'You're right,' he said to the woman who had just spoken. 'She does have a nest back there.' He smirked and cast a malevolent glance at Rose. 'Call yourself a tour-guide. Hah! Can't even see a crocodile when it's this close.'

Rose stared in amazement. Her entire boat-load was gazing happily at a rotting log on the riverbank, their cameras clicking, videos whirring, convinced it was a real-life crocodile. She opened her mouth to speak and then thought better of it. In stunned amazement she turned to Ryan, to find his dark eyes on hers, solemnly waiting.

'Can you see it now, Miss O'Meara?' he mocked.

All the tourists' attention was on the bank. Rose and Ryan were effectively alone.

'I'd be mad not to,' she said slowly.

'How wise.' His eyes filled with laughter. 'How very wise. If you're going to keep up this guided tour operation, you need to improve your crocodile-spotting skills.'

'Or just bring you with me,' she retorted. 'With your eyes we could find polar bears. . .'

'I've seen four this morning,' Ryan admitted, a smile lurking behind the grey of his eyes. 'No big ones, though. It must be the breeding season.'

Rose choked on a bubble of laughter and then caught herself swiftly as one of her tourists turned to ask her a question. It wouldn't do for her to laugh now. Her part was the dopey tour-guide, and if her tourists needed to think her stupid before they'd be happy, then she was happy to oblige. As they took their last photographs Rose gunned *Crocalook* into life and headed for home.

Ryan was the first off the boat as they approached the mooring. He took Rose's mooring-ropes and attached them to the jetty bollards, and by the time she had farewelled the last of her satisfied tourists he had gone, slipping unobtrusively back on to the *Mandala*.

It was just as well, Rose thought grimly. He had saved her a morning's fares, but her overwhelming feeling wasn't gratitude.

What was it, then? Resentment? Anger? Confusion? The last word was right. The man confused her. He only had to look at her to make her feel angry, and resentful and lonely and fearful and. . . And a million other conflicting emotions she could hardly put a name to.

Rose went up to the first-aid room and saw her five waiting patients for the day. There were four she could cope with herself—two bad sunburns, a cut which she could stitch, and an infected ear. She wrote a script which Steve would countersign next Monday. Lastly, just as she was about to go, a child was presented with excruciating stomach pains. Little Cathy Leishman was doubled over in agony. Her father carried her in, his face pale with concern.

'It's done it again, Doc,' he said brusquely.

Rose's heart sank. Cathy had a hernia which had come close to strangulating once before. She had managed to get it back into position and had strongly advised the Leishmans to have it seen to. That had been two months ago.

'You haven't seen anyone, I suppose,' she said grimly. 'I thought I told you. . .'

'It's been fine,' Ray Leishman expostulated. 'There hasn't been a need.'

'I told you this could happen,' Rose snapped. 'She should have had it repaired two months ago.' She took the child from Ray and laid her on the examining-couch. Baring the child's small abdomen, she bit her lip. She had managed to get the protruding bowel back last time. Could she do it again?

'Don't touch it,' Cathy sobbed. 'It hurts.'

'I know it does, little one,' Rose said softly. 'But I'll be quick. Just hold your breath and hold Daddy's hand tight while I see if I can stop it hurting.'

Her fingers moved gently but firmly, trying. It was harder than last time. The bowel had come further out. The child whimpered under her hands but finally, finally, the protruding piece of bowel slid back into position. Rose let her breath go. The last thing she could deal with was a true strangulating hernia. They had been lucky.

'OK,' she told the father as the little girl relaxed. 'I want Cathy taken up to Batarra now.' Batarra was the nearest centre with a surgeon, thirty miles to the south. 'That hernia needs to be repaired straight away. We've been lucky twice and I'm not risking a third time.'

'But it's fine,' Ray Leishman protested. 'Look at her.' Cathy was smiling at her mother and trying to sit up. 'You've done great, Doc.'

'The hole's extending,' Rose said. 'It'll happen again, and if the bowel blocks completely then Cathy's in real trouble.'

'Yeah, well, I'll make an appointment for her,' Ray said. 'But not this afternoon. I'm supposed to be working and the missus doesn't drive.'

'No.' Rose crossed to the telephone. 'I'll ring Batarra now and tell them to expect you. She has to go this afternoon. By ambulance if you can't take her.'

'But we haven't got ambulance insurance.'

'Then you'll have to take her yourself. Now, Mr Leishman.'

She left them grumbling, wishing more than anything that she had the necessary piece of paper to treat Cathy herself. A hernia repair was easy unless it was strangu-

lating. If she were qualified then the doctor from
Batarra would come down and assist her to operate.
As it was. . . Batarra's surgeon was elderly and his
surgery was questionable. She had no choice, however.
She saw the child off and made her way back to the
boat.

She had ten minutes to eat her lunch—a dry biscuit
and vacuum flask coffee—sitting on the deck of
Crocalook waiting for her afternoon tourists. She didn't
feel the least hungry. Sorrow was still washing over
her, leaving her feeling empty and nauseous, but she
had missed dinner and breakfast. She forced the food
down, all the time aware that Dr Ryan Connell was
only yards from her. The smoked windows of the
Mandala revealed nothing. She could have an audience
of hundreds for all she knew.

'He'll be up in his salon, drinking champagne and
eating caviare, I'll bet,' she said savagely to herself.
'He's had his fun at my expense. That'll be the last I
see of him.'

CHAPTER THREE

IT WAS the last she saw of him for four more hours.
Rose ran her afternoon cruise successfully, to her relief
this time finding a real crocodile. Afterwards she ran a
brief afternoon surgery, cleaned *Crocalook*, and then,
on impulse, spent an hour servicing the engine. After
all, there was no Pa waiting at home. There was
nothing waiting at home.

Finally she had done all she could to prevent a
recurrence of the morning's motor trouble and she rose
to leave. 'You can have the day off tomorrow,' she told
the little boat, leaving her advertising board face-down
on the deck instead of putting it out on the jetty.
'You've earned it.' She turned to find Ryan Connell
watching from the jetty.

'Dirty enough?' he queried mildly.

Rose flushed, glancing down at her clothes. She had
changed for afternoon surgery but she was filthy again,
now liberally covered in engine oil. 'It's dirt from an
honest day's work,' she snapped.

'You can't accuse me of being idle rich today.' He
smiled, his scarred face lighting with humour. 'I found
a crocodile.'

Rose choked on a sudden bubble of laughter, her
anger fading as her sense of humour reasserted itself.
'I'd love to see my tourists' faces when their photographs show mangrove seedlings sprouting from the
tail of their "crocodile".' She looked up at him self-
consciously. 'Thank you,' she faltered. 'It was kind. . .'

He stared down at her, an odd look on his face. 'I
don't usually do things to be kind,' he said softly.

'No?'

'No.' He hesitated. 'Not usually. Have you finished for the day?'

Rose nodded, unsmiling, her humour ebbing. What was it about this man that put her on the defensive?

He moved to take her arm as she walked up the ramp but she brushed him aside impatiently. 'Thanks, but I don't need help,' she told him.

'I can see that,' he agreed gravely. He hesitated again. 'Is the man in your life home making supper and warming your bedroom slippers?'

Rose stared at the man before her, and once again laughter caught her unawares as she realised what he was asking. 'No,' she told him. 'I don't have a house-husband—although I'd love one. . .' And then, as she thought of what lay waiting for her at home—emptiness and no one—her voice trailed off into silence. Oh, Pa. . .

Ryan saw her face change. His scarred brow twisted as he frowned. 'Now what have I said to hurt you?' he demanded swiftly. 'I didn't mean to open a can of worms.'

'There's no can of worms.' Rose's voice was bleak.

'Good.' He took her arm decisively, as if suddenly sure of his ground. 'My secretary has the night off and I've a meal for two. You can eat with me tonight.'

'Me?' Rose's voice rose on an involuntary squeak of surprise. 'Eat with you? You have to be kidding.'

'I never kid, Miss O'Meara. When you know me better you'll realise that.'

'I don't intend to get to know you better.' Rose drew her arm from his grasp and pulled herself to full height, searching for dignity. 'Dr Connell. . .'

'Ryan.'

'Dr Connell, you and I live in different worlds. We have nothing in common.' She looked down at her bare, oil-stained legs. 'I'll bet you have a whole lot of expensive furnishings in there I could ruin by just sitting on them.'

'Maybe I'd judge it worth the loss.'

Rose stared up at him. His eyes were suddenly intent. His mouth was twisted into a wry smile but his eyes were deadly serious.

'You, I gather, have been Kora Bay's medical officer for the last two years. I understand my arrival will put you out of a job.'

'You're qualified and I'm not,' she said briefly. 'End of discussion.'

'That's for me to say. I want you to come to dinner.'

'Not tonight,' she said unsteadily. She made to pass him but he put out a hand and stopped her. 'Let me go, please,' she protested. 'I need to go home and have a bath.'

'So the only thing stopping you accepting my invitation to dinner is your oil-slick?'

Despite her discomfiture, Rose grinned. This man had such a nice way of describing things. Her oil-slick. . .'It's a major drawback to elegant eating,' she smiled.

'Then allow me to assist,' Ryan said softly. Before Rose realised his intentions he dropped his hands to her waist and swung her strongly up into his arms. 'I have just the thing for stubborn oil-slicks.'

'Just the. . .' Rose gave an undignified yelp. 'What are you doing?' She writhed helplessly against him. 'Put me down.' At the other end of the jetty a group of tourists stopped to watch the goings-on of this odd couple. Their faces reflected interest and indulgent good humour. A lovers' spat?

'I will in a moment,' Ryan promised, his grip tightening around her slim body as he strode forward on to the *Mandala*. The vast mahogany doors were wide open. He didn't hesitate, but kept right on going.

Shock held Rose speechless. No man had ever touched her like this in her whole twenty-six years. No man would dare. What gave this man the right to sweep her off her feet and drag her into his den?

His den. That was where she was, she thought, her mind reacting in frantic panic. She should be screaming at the top of her lungs, screaming so that every tourist within a mile of the marina came running. So why wasn't she? Why was she silently submitting to being carried forward? She was submitting to the feel of his arms holding her body against his muscled frame. She was submitting to being taken. . .where?

To the bath. What little breath Rose had regained disappeared completely as she saw where he was taking her. They had crossed the big reception area and Ryan had pushed open a door with his foot as he moved swiftly forward. Rose had never seen anything like this. Not ever. . .

The bathroom was pure white, walled and floored with magnificent shimmering Italian tile. There were no mirrors. With these tiles there hardly needed to be. The whole room centred around the enormous bath. It was set deep into the floor, a pool of steaming, clear water just waiting to be used. Ryan flicked a switch with his shoulder as he entered and the whole bath rose into bubbles, hissing and steaming like a vast pot waiting for its offering.

Rose writhed against the man holding her, her mind whirling at what was happening. 'Put. . . Put me down,' she whispered. 'You can't. . .'

'You said you wanted a bath,' he told her reasonably. 'I'm offering you one.'

'I can't go in there. . .' The feel of Ryan's arms around her was doing strange things to Rose's body. Her voice sounded as though it didn't belong to her.

'Why not?' Ryan grinned wickedly down at the lady in his arms.

'I don't. . . I'm not dressed. . . I can't. . .' Rose choked incoherently and then fought for calm. 'I'd leave an oil-slick half an inch thick,' she squeaked. 'And I haven't clothes. . .'

'Problem one solved.' With his foot, Ryan pressed a

gold disc beside the bath. A stream of liquid shot into the bath and the bubbles immediately became foam. The foam built up and spilt in waves out over the tiled floor. 'Soap, my lady. Excellent for oil-slicks.' Then he crossed to the wall and took down a heap of pure white towelling. 'And problem two. One pair of towels and one bathrobe. Your clothes are dirtier than you are. Bathe with them on and then hang them out on deck. In this warm wind they'll dry while we eat dinner. . .'

'But I don't want to. . .'

'Bathe with them on?' He smiled, and his smile was pure Machiavellian. 'I agree you'd be more comfortable with nothing. But I imagine you might feel more comfortable with a protective layer or two around you.' His smile deepened. 'It might be wise at that. . .'

'How dare you. . .?' Rose wriggled and gasped as she felt his arms tightening. The feel of his body. . . 'Put me down,' she demanded breathlessly. 'This instant!'

'Are you sure?'

'Of course I'm sure!' Then, as he strode forward, Rose realised what he intended and let out an incredulous yelp. It was too late for yelps, though. It was too late for anything. Her body was gently lowered and released into the mound of warm, enveloping foam.

To her amazement, Rose's first reaction was pure, instinctive pleasure. The warm water enveloped her, and the soft, bubbling foam was like an embrace. Rose sank and then found her feet, standing with foam to breast height, and felt the bubbles caress her tired body. She looked up at the man standing above her and closed her eyes in disbelief. This wasn't happening to her.

She should have screamed. For the first time the enormity of her situation sank home. This man had her in his power. He could do anything he wished with her now and she was powerless to stop him. If she screamed, then she doubted if she could be heard on

the jetty outside—not if the thickness of those doors
was any indication of the strength of this boat's walls.
She looked up at Dr Ryan Connell, and for the first
time her face reflected fear.

He saw it. She saw the flash of recognition in his
eyes and she saw the quick negation of his head-shake.

'I'm not about to ravish you, Miss O'Meara,' he said
softly, looking down at her in her pool of bubbles. 'My
ambition is to get you clean and fed. If you have any
idea how much of a waif you look. . .'

'Like a stray dog,' Rose said bitterly.

'Something like that,' he agreed. 'Why do I have the
impression that you need some attention lavished on
you?'

'I don't,' Rose snapped. 'I can take care of myself,
thank you very much.' She felt totally out of her depth,
soaked in warm bubbles, with her breasts level to this
man's feet.

'OK, you don't.' Ryan smiled. He walked to the
bathroom door, and then turned back to face her. 'But
for tonight you're having it anyway. If you were going
to eat one dry cracker for lunch when you're as thin as
you are, then you should have done it out of my sight.
I could never bear the sight of a starving pup.' His
smile deepened. 'Especially one as lovely as Miss Rose
O'Meara.'

Rose fought for her voice. 'Dr Connell. . .'

'I'll leave you now,' he said soothingly. 'There's a
lock on your side of the door, but I can assure you
there's no need for it. You won't be disturbed. Dinner
is ready when you are, my lady.' He walked out of the
room, closing the door behind him.

For one long moment Rose stayed motionless in the
bath, staring at the closed door. What was happening?
Then, with a gasp, she hauled herself over the rim of
the bath on to the tiled floor and made a soggy dash
for the door. The lock slid home with a comforting
click, and Rose leaned against the closed door in relief.

She was alone. He couldn't come in. She couldn't leave either, but for the moment all that mattered was that Ryan Connell was on the other side of the door and she was alone.

She stared down at her clothes. Her shorts and disreputable T-shirt were covered in foam. She put a hand up to her nose and foam came away on her fingers.

A bubble bath. . . Rose had never had such a thing in her life. A bubble spa, she corrected herself suddenly, and despite herself she gave an involuntary chuckle. She looked ridiculous. A waif, Dr Connell had called her. A soggy waif, she corrected him, and suddenly lifted her arms and pulled her T-shirt over her head.

She was here now and she was already wet and half washed. If she screamed loud enough Ryan Connell would release her and she could go home, sodden and undignified, to her silent, memory-laden cottage. And if she stayed? If she stayed then she could soak in this magnificent tub to her heart's content, and for a while—just a while—she could put away the thought of her grandfather's death and the mound of bills waiting for her at home.

And she could have dinner with Dr Connell. . .

The knowledge of the biggest temptation of all flashed into her mind and she rejected it absolutely. Dr Ryan Connell was here to be used, she said to herself. He was rich and he could afford to indulge whims. Well, she was in the mood for whims, and she was simply using Ryan Connell and his wonderful boat to drive away the sorrow and worry of the past few months—of the next few days. She rid herself of the rest of her clothes and slid decisively back into the waiting foam.

Rose stayed in the bath for an hour. The water stayed steaming hot, and her body welcomed the soaking comfort like soothing balm. Below water level there was a seat that acted as a bed, with arm-rests and a smooth tiled head-rest. Rose lay back and let the bubbles do their work. Her mind emptied. She blocked the thought of her grandfather's death and her financial hassles. She blocked the thought of Ryan Connell. . .

Finally she was sated. Her fingers were shrivelling like prunes. She looked at them and smiled. The last of the oil-stains on her fingers had disappeared. She had never been so clean in all her life. She pulled her clothes into the bath with her and washed them as best she could—the oil-stains were fixed in them for life, she thought ruefully—and climbed reluctantly from the foam.

There was no further avoiding the outside world. She had to face things again. She had to face the empty cottage. But first she had to face Ryan Connell.

She towelled herself dry and wrapped her mass of dripping curls in one of Ryan's vast white towels. Then she wrapped herself in the big white bathrobe and took a deep breath.

She should pull on her sodden clothes and march right out of here. Say, 'Thank you very much for the bath, sorry I'm dripping on your carpet,' and march out of the door. Back to her empty cottage. . .

No. She couldn't do it. Not yet. She looked down at her bare pink toes and wriggled them tentatively. The sight gave her comfort and she grinned. She was a far cry from any woman Ryan Connell would be used to. A waif, he had called her. He feels sorry for me, she told herself firmly. I'm safe with him because all he feels for me is the sympathy of the rich for the underclass. The thought pushed the humour from her eyes, and gave her enough courage to walk to the door and open it.

Ryan was on the telephone, seated at the bar which opened on to the reception area. Rose stared around with interest, noting how the huge room could be swiftly turned into an efficient reception area with the closing of three sliding doors. Now. . .now it looked like a magnificent living-room.

Ryan smiled across at her with his eyes, motioned to a bottle of open champagne in a tub of ice and a waiting glass, and went back to his conversation. His tone was curt and businesslike. 'I want him back here as soon as possible,' he was saying. 'Now his lungs are clear there's no reason to hold him in Cairns. He's better off here.'

And then. . .'Yes, there are medical facilities at Kora Bay now. From here on we can cope with standard medicine locally.'

Rose flushed. From here on. . . From here on she wasn't wanted. Not by Kora Bay. And not by her grandfather.

Rose crossed to the table and lifted the bottle, eyeing it dubiously. Champagne. . . She placed it firmly back in the ice-bucket, went and sat on the comfortable club sofa as far from Ryan as she could manage and placed her hands nervously on her lap. She felt like a child who had wandered into the wrong classroom.

Ryan finished his telephone conversation two minutes later and replaced the receiver, then stood for a long moment looking across at the girl seated on his settee. His impression of a waif deepened. Rose's eyes were rimmed by shadows, and her hands were tightly gripped together. The self-confidence of yesterday had disappeared. Rose was totally out of her depth and it showed. He smiled and crossed to pour champagne into a glass. 'You don't drink?'

'No,' Rose told him. 'At least. . .'

'At least, not with me,' Ryan smiled. 'Very wise.' He crossed to where she sat. Uncertain, Rose stood, her hands gripping the folds of her bathrobe around her. It was respectable enough but underneath she was naked.

She felt naked. Ryan's eyes looked at her with a

warmth that once again acknowledged her as all woman.

'I told you,' Ryan said softly. 'I'm not about to ravish you.' His eyes took in the soft curves of her breast under her bathrobe, and her huge green eyes. He reached forward and loosened the towel around her hair. Damp red-brown curls cascaded out to fall in a mass around her shoulders.

'You heard what I was saying?' he asked, his eyes watching her intently.

'Yes.' She hesitated. 'Lenny Carter.'

'Yes.' He poured a glass of champagne and then stood staring into its bubbling depths. 'There was water on his lungs so I sent him down to Cairns. They've just rung to say he's all clear.'

'That's great,' Rose said stiffly.

'It is. Thanks to you.'

Rose shook her head. 'I. . .you would have coped.'

He shook his head. 'They wouldn't have known I was here, and in the time it would have taken to find out Lenny would have died. So the life saved is your responsibility.'

'I'll go out on a high note, then.' There was no disguising the bitterness in Rose's voice.

'What's your medical training?' Ryan demanded. 'If you're a trained nurse I could use you.'

'I told you.' Rose shook her head. 'I'm not qualified.'

'So why do they use you? You must have some medical training.' Ryan Connell frowned. 'And they call you Doc.'

'They shouldn't. I haven't the right.'

'So what is your training?' he demanded again. 'Did you start medical school?'

Rose got up then, and crossed to the window. Her hands were gripping themselves in a convulsive hold.

'I finished medical school,' she told the darkened window.

'Here? In Australia?'

'In Brisbane.'

'And passed?'

'Yes.'

There was a long silence. Then Ryan crossed to stand behind her. He grasped her shoulders and pulled her round to face him. 'Then why the hell are you playing crocodile-hunter instead of practising as a doctor?' he said roughly. 'It doesn't make sense.'

'I told you.' Rose's voice was a whisper. She didn't look up at him. She couldn't. 'I'm not qualified.'

'Well, why the hell not?'

'I haven't done my residency.'

His eyes snapped together as if trying to solve some impossible jigsaw. 'You did your entire medical training and didn't do your residency,' he said blankly.

'No.' Rose pulled away. 'I might. . . I might do it now. Now you're here.'

'Well, that's a great idea,' he said savagely. 'Why now?'

'Because I'm not needed here any more.'

'You mean. . .' He frowned. 'You mean you abandoned your medical course to provide Kora Bay with a half-trained medical officer?'

Rose stared up at him. His eyes were blank with astonishment. She couldn't explain, though. Not tonight. If she mentioned her grandfather to this man she would break down entirely.

'That's right,' she whispered. 'And. . . And I like crocodiles.'

'And tourists, I suppose,' he said drily, and Rose flushed.

'If you don't like tourists you won't make your living in Kora Bay,' she told him. 'They're half your work-load.'

'I can imagine.'

Rose frowned. She turned back to the sofa and sat, pulling her robe around her. 'Why. . .why are you here?' she asked tentatively. There were lots of things about this man that didn't make sense.

'I run a locum service along the coast,' Ryan told her brusquely. 'Your Roger Bain contacted me and asked if I was interested in setting up here permanently. I told him I'd give it a six-month trial.'

'But. . .' Rose turned this over in her mind. In Rose's experience locums were usually impecunious doctors between jobs. Not wealthy physicians—owners of cruisers. . .

'You don't. . .you're not usually a locum?'

'I am now.'

'But. . .'

'If you mean where did I earn enough money to buy the *Mandala* why don't you come out and say so?'

'OK.' Rose took a deep breath. 'Where did you earn enough money to buy the *Mandala*?'

'I practised as a physician for eight years in Brisbane.'

'So why did you leave?'

'That's my business.' His tone told her there were to be no more questions. He reached over and touched her hair. 'And now, Dr O'Meara. . .'

'I'm not. . .'

'If you've completed six years' medical school then you're a doctor, regardless of whether you're registered or not,' he said roughly. 'Now, let's leave our respective inquisitions. If you fail to comb your hair it's going to dry in a tangled knot.' His fingers ran down the nape of her neck, and Rose gave an involuntary shudder of pleasure. 'I suppose you haven't a brush.' Ryan fingered her curls. 'You really should carry a handbag, you know.'

'For all the occasions I get picked up and thrown bodily into baths,' Rose responded. She had been trying for sarcasm but her voice was breathless. The feel of his fingers through her hair was doing strange things to her. 'My hair's fine.'

'No.' Ryan left her, striding swiftly across the room to another door. Seconds later he was back, a tortoise-shell brush and comb in his hand. 'Sit,' he ordered.

'My hair's fine,' Rose repeated. She stood and backed away. 'It doesn't matter if it dries like this. It only tangles again in the wind on the boat.'

'Which explains your usual very flattering hairstyle,' Ryan said grimly. 'Dr O'Meara, sit—or would you like to be sat?'

'S. . . Sat?'

'Sat.' Ryan advanced threateningly. 'Picked up and placed on your very attractive bottom. Sat. The choice is yours.'

Rose looked up at his face and knew he spoke the truth. This man was not used to making idle threats. She chose to sit.

It was the strangest feeling, submitting to Ryan Connell's care. Rose had not been near a hairdresser for years, and she had forgotten what it felt like, though maybe she wouldn't feel like this with a hair-dresser touching her hair. Ryan Connell was no hair-dresser. He was an arrogant, male, chauvinistic, rich. . .

Her adjectives ran out as the feel of Ryan Connell's fingers through her hair took over. It was as if she had nerves exposed at every root of every hair, and each nerve was sending searing messages to the rest of her body as it was touched. Her hair felt alive. Her body felt. . . She shifted involuntarily on her seat as she tried to come to terms with these unfamiliar sensations. Ryan's hands moved with her and the feeling intensified.

For so many years now Rose had been the carer. Since she had returned from university her grandfather had desperately needed her. There was no one to pamper her—no money to spend on her and no one to turn to with her mountain of worries.

For this moment—for this instant of time and regardless of whether it had any foundation in fact—Rose felt cherished. She felt like a woman who was loved and cared for and treasured for herself. It was a dream, she thought lazily, a strange, surreal dream that would stop in a moment as this man's hands stopped their ministrations. But for now. . .

But for now she would sink into the dream and let these fingers to their worst. She lay back in the armchair and closed her eyes. Ryan's fingers skilfully combed the knots from her curls and then placed the comb aside. The fingers came back to her head and started massaging softly, softly and then with a greater intensity, as if the fingers knew that Rose was theirs— that Rose was lost in the feeling those fingers were sending through her body.

The fingers ceased abruptly and it was all Rose could do not to cry out a protest.

'To tie this up with twine is criminal,' Ryan was saying roughly, and to Rose's surprise his voice was not quite steady. It was as if some of the feelings she was experiencing had imparted themselves to him. She looked up at him and then swiftly away. Her body was betraying her, and the look of him was enough to send her emotions tumbling over the edge. What on earth was wrong with her? Ryan Connell was only a man, and a man she didn't like. Why couldn't she meet his look?

'Where are your clothes?' Ryan asked abruptly, as if searching for some other focus for his attention than this frail slip of a girl with her too large eyes.

'In. . . In the bathroom.'

'I'll put them outside to dry.'

'I'll do it.' Rose stood shakily, and as she did her foot caught in the fold of her long bathrobe. She stumbled and would have fallen, but Ryan was too fast. In one swift movement he had her, his arms supporting her until she found her balance.

'I can see why you don't drink champagne,' he said, and his voice was suddenly husky.

For one long moment Rose couldn't respond. Her breasts were tight against his chest. The feel of him was sending shards of fire through her. She should be pulling away. She should. . .

She gave a gasp of dismay and pulled back, away from his arms. His hands lingered on her arms, as though reluctant to release their captive.

'I. . . I think I'd better go,' Rose faltered. 'I don't need. . .'

'You need dinner,' Ryan said softly, his voice steadying as he saw her indecision. 'Or am I wrong? Do you have a roast dinner with vegetables waiting for you at home?'

'N. . . No.'

'Well, then.' He smiled down at her and his smile made Rose's heart lurch within her. That smile. . . Despite the scar that ran down the side of his face, Ryan's smile had the capacity to warm and to caress. She looked up at him and her world twisted in confusion. What was happening to her?

Her arms were released, as if Ryan had come to a decision. He walked across to the bathroom and retrieved her damp shorts and shirt from where she had placed them. He also picked up one pair of panties and a bra. Rose's face burned with embarrassment and she moved across to take them from him.

'I'll hang them out,' she said swiftly.

'Just be careful where you put them then,' Ryan grinned. 'I have my reputation to consider.'

'I wouldn't imagine your reputation would be damaged one bit by having the odd bra hanging over your decking,' Rose said unsteadily.

He raised his brows again. 'Your opinion of me is not too high, is it, Dr O'Meara?'

Despite her confusion, Rose smiled. 'I'll reserve any opinion of your character until after you've fed me.'

She took a deep breath. 'You're right, Dr Connell. I'm hungry.'

He raised his hands and smiled. 'OK, Dr O'Meara. Hint taken. I'll start cooking now.'

The cooking, however, was doomed to wait. As Ryan turned away from her a shout brought him up short.

'Doctor. . .' The yelling came from outside the boat. 'Doctor. . . Please. . .'

CHAPTER FOUR

'DOCTOR!' The call came again, this time more urgent. There was fear in the word. Ryan grimaced. 'My call, I think,' he said.

'I'm still supposed to be working until Monday,' Rose ventured, and Ryan grinned.

'You're hardly dressed for working,' he suggested. He stepped through the big doors out on to the deck.

He left the door open and Rose could hear every word. The conversation carried across the water of the estuary on the still night and she grimaced at what she was hearing.

'Dr Connell?'

'Yes.' Ryan's voice was clipped, smooth and professional. There was no rudeness at being interrupted. He could hear the urgency behind the tone.

It was a man's voice talking and Rose had no difficulty in recognising Ray Leishman, Cathy's father.

'We can't find Doc O'Meara,' Ray said hoarsely. 'And Cathy. . .my kid. . . She's real bad.'

With a gasp of dismay Rose tightened her bathrobe around her and stepped out on to the deck. At any other time Ray Leishman would have been shocked to the core. Now. . . Now it said a lot for his level of concern that his eyes held only relief. 'Rose,' he said hoarsely. 'I've been looking everywhere. . . It's Cathy. . .'

'Didn't you take her up to Batarra?'

'I should have,' the man groaned. 'The wife wanted me to. But I thought. . . Well, I was that busy. I rang up and changed the appointment to tomorrow.'

'And now she's worse.'

'Yeah. She. . .she's sick as a dog. . . Honest, Rose, I know you warned us but it seemed so easy to get the

55

thing back in. I decided you were interfering with a man's work for nothing. But now. . . Now, she's gone all quiet and limp. She seems worse than the last two bouts. Can you come and fix her up again?'

Could she come. . . Rose thought of how lucky she had been the last two times and angry words died on her lips. Of all the stupid, criminal negligence. . .

If the bowel was strangulating. . . Rose took a deep breath, trying to control her anger and fear. Swiftly she told Ryan what had happened, her mind racing while she talked.

If she couldn't get it back. . . It was a dirt road to Batarra—nearly a two-hour drive. To a child who sounded as if she was already in shock. . .

'It sounds as if we might have to operate here, then,' Ryan said grimly as Rose finished talking, and Rose turned to stare at him.

'Operate here?' She shook her head. 'We haven't the facilities. We're just going to have to get her to Batarra as fast as possible.'

'We can operate on board,' Ryan snapped. 'We'll have to get her to hospital in Batarra, though. If I operate then she'll need intensive nursing, and I haven't nursing facilities yet. We can get to Batarra by boat while we operate. It'll be an easier journey than by road afterwards. Batarra's on the coast and the water between here and there is calm enough for our purposes. I need to get Roy back, though. He was having dinner at the pub.'

'Roy. . .'

'My secretary-cum-deck-hand-cum-navigator.' He looked up at Ray Leishman. 'Where's the child?'

'She's in the car. At the marina car park.'

'Carry her down here now. With a bit of luck we might be able to get the damned thing back. I'll telephone the hotel and locate Roy while you bring her down—just in case.'

* * *

There was no way the bowel could be repositioned. It was protruding twice as far as the last time Rose had seen it. She looked at the bulge emerging from the stomach wall and her heart sank.

Ryan's fingers moved carefully over the swollen area, but not for long. He raised his head and shook it. 'We're wasting time,' he said softly. 'The bowel will die if we leave it any longer, and I don't fancy a resection on a child as ill or as young as this. Let's go, Dr O'Meara.'

'But. . .'

He fixed her with a look. 'Can you give an anaesthetic?' he demanded. He was treating her as if she were deliberately wasting time.

'I. . . I've only ever given one under supervision.'

'Well, now you're going to give one on your own. There's a first time for everything.'

'But the Medical Board. . .'

'Leave the Medical Board to me. Let's move.'

It was the strangest operation ever, Rose thought later, and yet, in another sense, it was amazingly normal. Ryan showed her the small theatre on board and Rose was taken aback by its facilities. It was designed for minor surgery—lacerations and so on—but Ryan Connell had clearly thought of the fact that it might be used for full-scale surgery when he designed it.

Rose went over and over the anaesthetic procedure as Ryan meticulously prepared his equipment and then scrubbed. She did it aloud, and Ryan prompted her as she went. Finally he nodded.

'You'll do,' he said brusquely. 'Let's go.'

So while Cathy's parents sat in the luxurious waiting-room and while Roy, the middle-aged man Ryan's phone call had brought hurrying back to the boat, steered them out of the harbour and along the sheltered inner reef waters to Batarra, Ryan Connell performed his first surgery as Kora Bay's doctor.

He was good. Rose had seen enough operations in her student days to recognise skill when she saw it, and she knew that Cathy Leishman was lucky to have him.

The child had need of luck. Ryan laid bare the bowel, extending the gap from where it protruded to ease the constriction. Without its slight cover of flesh and skin, the savage purple of the bowel showed just how serious the situation really was.

Rose glanced down at the angry mass and bit her lip. Were they too late? If the bowel was dead. . . She thought of resection procedures and cringed inwardly.

Ryan had warm saline packs ready and Rose wondered at his skill as she turned back to concentrate on her anaesthesia. Maybe if she was more experienced she could have been of more use to Ryan, but as it was. . . As it was the shocked Cathy was close to death, and Rose needed every piece of knowledge about paediatric anaesthesia she had ever been taught. It was taking all Rose's skill to keep the flow adjusted, treading the fine line between keeping the child asleep and not burdening the child's failing body with too much of the drugs she was administering.

She could only marvel with a small section of her mind at Ryan Connell's skill. His injured hand didn't seem to impede him—in fact it was as if he forgot that it was injured as he worked. His twisted hand followed his orders as if by magic.

To perform the surgery he was doing in these conditions—in a cramped theatre with no nursing staff at all, with the deck moving slightly beneath him as the *Mandala* made its swift way to Batarra. . . Rose thought back to the array of back-up available to the surgeons in her student days. . . Skilled anaesthetists specially trained in children's anaesthesia, an assisting surgeon and three or four nurses to see everything was on hand as it was needed. Now. . .

Ryan had pre-prepared everything and had forgotten nothing. His hands moved swiftly and he even had time to glance up at Rose every now and then—time to flash her a glance of reassurance that she was doing the right thing.

'I think. . . I think we might have done it,' he said softly, and Rose glanced briefly again at the bowel. And again. There was no mistaking what was happening. The section of bowel was changing its colour. The purple was fading slowly to a healthy, living pink.

'Oh, thank God,' she whispered.

Rose felt her heart swell in satisfaction as Ryan closed. If this operation had been performed at a main Australian children's hospital it could not have been done better.

Rose watched the bowel being repositioned with a small nod of satisfaction. She looked down to the dials. Everything was OK. The child would live and the bowel would not require resection. Despite her father's stupidity.

'I think we can reverse now, Doctor,' Ryan said evenly and Rose flushed. He was finishing stitching and was about to dress the wound—the easy part—and it would have been appropriate for him to take over the more complex anaesthetic reversal. He saw no need, and that in itself was a bigger compliment than praise.

An ambulance met them at Batarra wharf. Ryan accompanied Cathy and her parents to hospital and Rose was left on the boat with Roy.

Roy was a quiet, self-effacing man, who seemed almost overwhelmingly shy. One leg seemed to be permanently damaged. He limped into the cabin as the ambulance departed and Rose started the unpleasant job of cleaning up. In his arms he carried a bundle of clothing Rose recognised.

'I'll do that,' he assured her. 'I've done it before and I know where the cleaning things are. These. . . I assume these are yours, miss,' he managed. 'They. . .

they were hanging out on deck when we left Kora Bay. . .'

Her clothes. Rose accepted the still damp clothes, almost rigid with embarrassment. She went back into the bathroom to change. When she returned Roy had finished the cleaning, firmly closed the door of the little theatre and was mixing a drink.

'I took the liberty of making you a juice cocktail,' he told her. 'It's not alcoholic. I. . . I thought you deserved it.'

How much did this quiet man know about her? Rose wondered. He had spent the evening in the Kora Bay hotel and Rose knew the medical happenings in Kora Bay were a subject of gossip. How much did those calm, kindly eyes know?

She took the drink gratefully. 'I. . .you must find it odd. . .' she started, and then stopped. How on earth did one explain one's lack of clothes?

'I don't find it anything,' he said calmly. 'Seems it was lucky you were on the boat when you were. I couldn't have done what you've done, though I've been called on to help in an emergency before.'

'You've been working for Dr Connell for a while?' Rose ventured, and Roy nodded.

'You could say that,' he said drily. 'Though only on the boat for a couple of years. Before that I worked on the doc's farm.'

'He has a farm?'

'He had a farm.' Roy poured himself a drink. 'It was his uncle's place—a big run about two hundred miles inland from Brisbane. Doc Connell used to work in Brisbane and fly home at weekends.'

Rose frowned. This wasn't making sense. 'Why. . . why did he leave Brisbane?' she asked.

Roy looked pensively at the girl seated before him. To talk or not to talk, his eyes seemed to be saying, and finally he gave a hint of a smile and a small decisive nod. It was as if he had come to some decision, and the decision was important.

'The homestead on the farm burned,' he said brusquely. 'That was the night Doc got burned.' He grimaced and motioned to his leg. 'And I scored this. After. . . Well, after he quit practice in Brisbane and moved on to the boat. I thought he intended to give up work entirely but he got sick of himself pretty damned fast. We pulled into a place one day and found a kid near-dead from a snake bite. The only doctor for a hundred miles was having a week's holiday. Doc pulled her through, spent a bit more money fitting the boat out, and started the locum service.' He stared into his drink. 'He hasn't enjoyed moving from one place to another, though. Seems Kora Bay might be where we'll settle for a while.'

'I see.' There were many things Rose didn't see, but they weren't things she could ask of Ryan Connell's employee.

'Tell me about Kora Bay?' Roy asked gently, his eyes on Rose's shadowed face. 'If we stay, will I enjoy it?'

'Oh, yes.' Roy had touched on the subject closest to Rose's heart and the trouble in her eyes faded for a little as she talked. By the time Ryan returned, Rose thought she had found a friend.

Roy disappeared almost as soon as Ryan arrived. 'I'll take her back to Kora Bay, will I?' he'd asked, and Ryan nodded.

'As quick as you can, Roy,' he told him. 'Kora Bay's without a doctor.'

'It's been without a doctor for years,' Rose said softly. 'Until you came.'

Ryan shook his head. 'No way,' he told her. His eyebrows twisted as he fixed her with a look. 'You might not have a piece of paper to prove it, but you're a damned fine doctor, Rose O'Meara. You should be

.

practising—not wasting your time on some crazy tourist indulgence.'

She wouldn't be wasting her time much longer. Rose looked bleakly up at Ryan and shook her head. His face changed.

'Now what the hell. . .?'

'I like my crocodiles,' she said stiffly. 'And I don't want to talk about it. If you don't mind. . .'

He stared at her for a long moment and then slowly nodded. 'As you wish.'

'Cathy was all right?'

'Safely bedded down for the night with intravenous antibiotics and constant nursing. She'll make it.'

'Thanks to you.'

Ryan shook his head. 'I couldn't have done it without you.' He grinned down at her. 'Clothes still wet?'

Rose flushed. 'I. . . No. They're fine.'

'Hungry?'

Rose took a deep breath. 'Yes,' she said definitely. 'Yes, I am.'

'So am I,' he agreed. 'And our dinner still waits.'

So as the *Mandala* sped smoothly along the calm coral sea back to Kora Bay, Rose was wined and dined in style.

Rose's opinion of the opulence of Ryan Connell's lifestyle was not changed by the meal he prepared. He had told her before she bathed that dinner was ready when she was, and she'd decided that it must be cold meat and salad. It was no such thing. Maybe Ryan Connell didn't know what a simple meal was.

They ate seafood—a simple scallop salad to start and then rock-oysters, crusted in a mound of ice and dripping lemon with a tartare sauce that tasted of tarragon and basil. Ryan drank wine and watched the girl before him sip her fruit cocktail. They talked little. Rose was unsure what to say, and Ryan Connell seemed content to watch.

He was a man who was good at watching, Rose

decided. His eyes saw everything. They noted the trouble she had with an oyster, crusted too far into its bed of ice and his fingers were there, chipping away the ice before she could even acknowledge that she was in trouble. He seemed intent on making her at ease. That he failed to succeed wasn't his fault. If only those eyes weren't so. . . Weren't so. . .

Rose didn't know. As Ryan cleared the dishes from the entrées she watched him silently as he moved around the kitchen area. He seemed almost as alone as she and yet so much more powerful. She found herself wondering again about the burns on his face and hand. They had been gained the night his farm had burned — but how? They seemed so much a part of the man that she now hardly noticed them, but she would like to know. . .

She couldn't ask. There was something about Ryan Connell that precluded questions. This was his good deed for the month, she decided, giving the impoverished tour boat operator-cum-student doctor a magnificent feed. After this he'd have nothing to do with her again.

Therefore she didn't need to know how he had been burned. She didn't need to know anything about him. She didn't need him to be any closer to her than he was now.

They headed into Kora Bay as Ryan produced the main course. Through the big windows Rose saw Roy secure the boat. He put his head in the door briefly.

'I'm off now, Doc,' he told Ryan. 'I'm sleeping at the pub for the night.' He smiled at Rose. 'I'll see you soon, I expect.' He grinned at her.

'Roy's a landlubber at heart,' Ryan told Rose as he came towards the table, bearing two huge plates. 'Any chance he can he gets off the boat and stays off.'

Rose smiled. She looked down at the plate Ryan set before her and her smile faded.

'Mud-crabs,' Ryan smiled, mistaking her silence for

confusion. 'I gather they're a delicacy in these parts. I've done them in a chilli sauce so I hope you're not averse to a bit of heat.'

'Chillied mud-crab. . .' Rose stared at the magnificent red crustacean on her plate and suddenly reality crashed back in on her. Dr Connell, his magnificent boat, and the events of the last few hours had managed to drive away the loneliness and the heartache for a little, but now they came flooding back to overwhelm her. She took a mouthful of the wonderful food and it almost choked her.

Mud-crab. . . Mud-crabs with chilli sauce had been her grandfather's favourite food. He had loved it with a passion and Rose had promised to make it for him the night he died. The crabs she had bought were still sitting uselessly on her kitchen table. . .

Ryan was staring down at her, his face expressionless. 'You don't like mud-crabs?'

'I. . . I do.' Rose looked up at him, her eyes brimming with unshed tears. 'I do. I just can't. . .'

She pushed her chair back abruptly and stood up. 'Look, I'm sorry,' she said shakily. 'I really am sorry, Dr Connell. You've been very kind but. . . But I shouldn't be here.'

Ryan moved towards her, his eyes a question, but Rose shook her head bleakly. Her mind was numb. How could she have enjoyed herself? How could she have let herself forget? She took a step towards the door and Ryan moved to take a grip on her arms.

'Do you mind telling me what the hell is going on?' he demanded.

Rose shook her head. 'I'm sorry,' she said bleakly. She should tell him, she thought, but the words wouldn't form in her mouth. To tell him about her grandfather. . . If she did she would break down completely, she knew. She would sob in his arms. The temptation to do just that was almost overwhelming, but she had just sufficient pride to hold her fragile control in place.

'Just accept that I'm allergic to mud-crab,' she said bleakly. 'Or maybe that mud-crab is a good food for bringing me to my senses.' She shook herself free of his arms. 'Thank you for the bath and for the food,' she told him. 'And thank you for Cathy. Goodnight.'

He was staring at her, his dark eyes blank. Then he frowned.

'Have you just decided to be loyal to a boyfriend?' he demanded. 'Is there some local hick who'd object to your dining in style?'

Rose flushed, her temper coming to her aid. 'That's right,' she said quietly. If he'd believe that, then so much the better. He'd want to be rid of her as much as she wanted to be off Ryan Connell's boat. 'My boyfriend and I eat mud-crab every night before we make love. It's an old Kora Bay custom.' She stepped back from him and started to turn away, but Ryan was before her, taking her arm and twisting her to face him.

'I told you,' he said savagely. 'I don't intend to ravish you. I invited you here because I felt sorry for you. . .'

'Well, I don't need your sympathy,' Rose snapped. 'And I don't need your mud-crab.'

'Because you can't eat it without making love?' Ryan demanded. 'What the hell. . .?'

'Of course I can eat it. . .' Rose broke off, her face suddenly crimson as she realised where her protests were leading her. 'Goodbye, Dr Connell.'

'Just a moment.'

Rose paused, her breath coming fast and her breasts heaving with emotion. She was so close to tears. . .

'Yes?' she said tightly. She was facing the door, away from the man behind her.

He took her shoulders in his grasp and turned her towards him. Rose pulled back, but her efforts were futile. Ryan Connell's grip was iron.

'You had one mouthful of my mud-crab,' he said slowly. 'And I'm not about to break a custom of Kora Bay. It's a rule of mine never to break local traditions if I can help it.' His grip tightened. He looked down at the flushed and angry face of the girl in his hold and he bent and kissed her.

Rose froze. The touch of Ryan Connell's mouth on hers was like some sorcerer's wand that paralysed—a feather touch that burned her entire being into absolute stillness. Rose's body petrified as his lips met hers. Her heart ceased beating within. What. . . What was happening to her?

And then, as the paralysis passed, the fire began. The kiss was deepened—the feather touch changing as the man holding her responded to the yielding softness of her flesh. The kiss became suddenly a command to respond, a demanding kiss that held her in thrall, that seared her lips, seared her heart, seared her very soul. . .

She should fight. . . She should fight and run. . . Rose could do neither. Her body was melting, a languid, drifting, sensuous warmth enveloping her, turning her legs to water and her will to nothing.

This wasn't happening to her. This was someone else being kissed. It was someone else responding to the feel of his lips, someone else lifting her hands to run her fingers sensuously through Ryan's coarse, sun-bleached hair, someone else parting their lips to let the searching tongue run over the white smoothness of her teeth.

It was someone else who moaned softly and pressed themselves closer as the kiss grew deeper, deeper. . . and the fire lit deep within her thighs and slowly spread. . .

But then, as the kiss finally drew to an end as all kisses eventually had to, and Ryan drew back and looked down at her with dark, fathomless eyes, the someone else was left behind. Rose's sorrow was still

there. This man could almost make her forget. . .
Almost, but it was too raw and new a grief.

Rose O'Meara looked up at Ryan, her eyes wide
with confusion and filled suddenly with unshed tears.
She gave a sob of pure confusion, and she turned from
Ryan Connell and fled.

CHAPTER FIVE

ROSE forced herself to stay in bed late the next day. She was more weary than she had ever been in her life before, wrung out with the emotion of the last two days. Sleep wouldn't come, but at least lying in her little back bedroom she could close her eyes and blot out the outside world.

Her grandfather's funeral was at ten a.m. At least it was this morning, she thought drearily. By lunchtime it would be over.

The events of the night before drifted through and through her mind, superimposing themselves on her grief. Too much had happened too fast. If she had met Dr Ryan Connell at another time. . .

If she'd met him at another time he never would have got near her, she acknowledged to herself. She would never have put herself in the situation of last night. To let a man take control of her. . .

Rose shook her head bleakly into the dawn light, her mind numb. She had reacted to him as she had reacted to no man before, but how much of that was due to the way she was feeling—to the overwhelming loneliness that was engulfing her?

'All of it,' she said savagely to the ceiling. 'All of it. Ryan Connell is nothing to me. He kissed me when I most needed human contact, and if I let him kiss me, it was just my loneliness that wanted him.'

It wasn't the truth. She knew that absolutely, and the knowledge frightened her half to death. Her mind had not reacted to Ryan Connell in loneliness. Her mind and her body had reacted with sheer animal pleasure and desire. Desire. . . She turned the word over in her tired mind and gave a sob of confusion. If that kiss had lasted a moment longer. . .

She pulled the pillow from under her head and buried her face in it, blocking the memory of the kiss from her brain. It refused to be blocked. The feel of Ryan's demanding lips on her mouth had burned into her heart and was there. . .was there for life?

'No!' It was a frightened wail, as if Rose were much younger than her twenty-six years. She felt about twelve. 'Oh, Pa,' she whispered into the dark. 'Where are you when I need you? You'd tell me what to do.'

She knew once more, though, that she was lying. Pa couldn't have told her what to do now. Or maybe he would. 'He's not our sort of folk, girl,' he might have said. 'He's big-city flash. He has money and power and probably as many women as he wants. What the hell does he want with a girl like you? He's dangerous, girl. Be civil, but keep your distance.'

'I will, Pa,' she said bleakly into the silence. 'I will. It's the only sensible thing to do.' The decision gave her no pleasure at all.

Shortly before ten Rose got up and dressed. Her wardrobe boasted one good outfit: a simple skirt and jacket she had bought at a sale for weddings and funerals. She put it on, frowning a little at its drab, outmoded appearance.

I would have liked to be pretty for Pa's funeral, she thought sadly, and then shook her head at her reflection in the mirror. In her grubby shorts and bare feet, Pa had thought her beautiful. He'd hated the serviceable skirts and blouses she wore for surgery and dresses, in his opinion, were silly gear. 'Wind catches 'em—you can't climb on a boat in 'em—what the hell do you want dresses for, my Rose?' He'd have been happier if she wore shorts to his funeral, Rose knew, but she wouldn't upset the small town conventions that much.

She brushed her hair until it shone, leaving it wild and free the way Pa loved it, and then, as she heard a car pull into the driveway, she walked to the door. The undertaker had promised to collect her in the funeral car that would follow the hearse. She opened the door and it wasn't the undertaker. It was Ryan Connell, standing on her front porch, his eyes black with anger.

Shock held Rose speechless. She stared stupidly up at the man before her, her mind considering and rejecting things to say in swift succession. What was she supposed to say? Good morning? How are you, Dr Connell? How may I help you? She said nothing, her mind trapped and silent with shock.

'Have you any idea what time it is?' Ryan Connell's voice was pleasant, but his eyes were wrathful.

Rose stared up at him, trying to make herself think. What on earth was driving the man?

'Y. . .yes,' she stammered. She looked down at her watch. 'Of course. It's just before ten. . .'

'Just before ten,' he said savagely. 'Just woken up, have we, Dr O'Meara?'

His anger broke through Rose's confusion. She tilted her chin and took a deep breath. 'Why are you here, Dr Connell?' she managed.

'I'm here to revoke your rights to my jetty,' he snapped. 'I told you I don't mind sharing the jetty as long as your tourists keep off my boat. For the second time in two days I've had tourists crawling all over the *Mandala* because the operator of O'Meara Croc Cruises can't get out of bed on time.'

Rose gasped. 'That's not fair. . .'

'Isn't it?' he said harshly. 'I've been tied up at the jetty for two mornings and both those mornings you managed to be late for your cruise.' He looked down at her serviceable skirt and blouse. 'Or not turn up at all. Having a day on the town, are we, Dr O'Meara?'

Rose flushed. There was no mistaking Ryan Connell's opinion of her dress. His scorn lent her courage, though. She glared up at him, her anger building to match his.

'I had no tourists booked for this morning,' she said firmly. 'And last night I left my sign face-down on my boat. There was nothing advertising a cruise this morning as I didn't intend to run one.'

Ryan frowned. 'How professional is that?' he snapped. 'To run a cruise when you feel like it. . .' Then, as he saw her open her mouth to interject, he raised a hand to silence her. 'I assumed in the. . .in the emotion of last night you'd forgotten to put your sign out. I saw it face-down on your boat and placed it on the jetty for you.'

Rose drew in her breath. 'How kind,' she snapped. 'How very kind. You interfere with the running of my business and then accuse me of interfering with yours. Did my tourists wake you up, then? Is the pampered Dr Connell intending to sleep until Monday morning when he condescends to start work?'

'Maybe it's you who is pampered,' Ryan said savagely. He stood, a dark, angry shadow, blocking the light from the fierce morning sun behind him. 'Today's Friday. I'd assume it's one of the busiest tourist days in Kora Bay. To fail to run a cruise because you don't feel like it. . .'

'It has nothing to do with you when I run or don't run my cruises.' Rose's green eyes were flashing daggers. 'My business has nothing to do with you. My life has nothing to do with you, so butt out, Dr Ryan Connell. Get back to your fancy boat and your fancy way of running a medical practice and leave me alone. . .'

'I'd do that if I thought I could be left in peace,' Ryan said savagely. 'You've been nothing but trouble. . .'

'I!' Rose gasped on the word, her anger building in its injustice. 'Of all the. . .'

'Dr O'Meara?'

Rose stopped in mid-tirade. Unnoticed, the undertaker's big black car had pulled up behind them. The undertaker was standing beside it, his hands respectfully folded, waiting for a chance to speak. Now he coughed politely. 'I'm sorry to interrupt, Dr O'Meara, but it's close on ten. We should be going.'

Rose looked wildly across at the undertaker, totally confused. She had been ready. She had been conditioning herself for this moment for two days, to enter the undertaker's car and go to bury her grandfather, but now all she felt was anger and confusion and helplessness.

All this must have shown on her face as the undertaker walked a little closer. He smiled professionally and smoothly, and held out a hand to Ryan Connell in greeting. 'I'm Henry Blake, from Blake's Funeral Home,' he said politely. 'I'm pleased to see Dr O'Meara has some company. I was a little concerned at her being alone at her grandfather's funeral. Most of our mourners have at least some family.'

Ryan's face changed in one swift, incredulous movement. His eyes swung to Rose. 'What the. . .?'

Rose shook her head, walking forward towards the waiting car. 'Dr Connell's not with me,' she said tremulously. All at once she was very close to tears. 'Thank you, Mr Blake. I'm ready.'

The undertaker looked uncertainly at her, and then back to Ryan. 'If you're sure. . .' he began.

'Your grandfather,' Ryan said slowly.

The undertaker saw Ryan's shock and reacted with professional ease to the situation as he now saw it. He had assumed this man was a close friend. A lover, he had decided, as he had heard them arguing. Well, maybe he was wrong, but Henry Blake sure as heck would like someone sitting in the mourner's car with this big-eyed slip of a girl. He liked there being someone with his principal mourner. If the girl was to collapse in grief then it wouldn't be Henry Blake who had to deal with it.

'Dr O'Meara's grandfather died the night before last,' he told Ryan smoothly. 'He was all the family the doctor had. Kept themselves to themselves, the two of them. And now. . .' He gestured helplessly at Rose's retreating back.

Rose was crying now, anger and sorrow mixing indiscriminately. The undertaker's words had been soft, meant for Ryan's ears and not hers, but she had heard them regardless. How dared Henry Blake expose her so? How dared he. . .?

It wasn't anger at Henry Blake that was causing this turmoil of emotion within her. It was anger at herself. Henry Blake hadn't exposed her. She was exposed already, raw in her grief and totally out of her depth in what she was feeling towards Ryan Connell. She was wide open to being hurt and the hurt was all around her. There couldn't be any pain worse than she was feeling now.

'Can we. . .can we go?' she pleaded. She looked back at Henry Blake, her big eyes brimming with unshed tears. Her eyes met Ryan Connell's, though, and she caught frantically at her fragile control. 'I'm sorry you were disturbed this morning, Dr Connell,' she said weakly. 'It won't happen again. I. . . The circumstances. . .' She broke off, unable to continue.

'Hell!' Ryan Connell's anger was still there but all of a sudden it was self-directed. He walked forward and gripped Rose's hands in his, ignoring her involuntary reaction to pull away. 'Why the hell didn't you tell me? Of all the crazy. . . I could have. . .'

'There was nothing you could do,' Rose told him with an attempt at dignity. 'You helped me to forget for a little while last night and for that I'm grateful. Please let me go now, Dr Connell.'

His hands retained their grip. He was looking down at her but Rose didn't meet his eyes. Instead she let

her gaze fall on to his hands, the one brown and
unscarred, and the other twisted and puckered with
scars.

Ryan Connell had seemed self-conscious about his
scarring the first time she had met the man. He wasn't
now. The twisted hand imparted strength and warmth,
telling her that, for this moment, she wasn't alone. The
awful bleakness lifted just a little, and as it did a tear
from Rose's brimming eyes swelled and fell, to land on
the tanned skin of his damaged hand.

Ryan stared down, and as he did his face twisted.
With his good hand he touched the teardrop on his
burned fingers, and then he regained his grip. 'You
really are doing this alone,' he said softly.

Rose still didn't look at him. She couldn't. What was
it about this man that made her want to cry?

'I have to,' she said bleakly. 'Please, Dr Connell.
Will you let me go?'

'Will you let me come with you?' Then, as Rose's
face changed, Ryan pulled her in to him and took her
shoulders in his grip. 'I should have known,' he said
savagely. 'The look. . .' He tilted her chin, forcing her
tear-laden eyes up to his. 'Believe me, Rose. You need
someone else today and if there's no one. . .' He shook
his head and then turned to Henry. 'We're ready.'

Rose gave an uncertain shake of her head. 'No,' she
faltered. 'You can't come. . . You're not. . .'

'I'm not dressed for a funeral?' Ryan looked ruefully
down at his tailored trousers and crisp linen shirt. 'I
suppose not. . .'

'You'll be fine,' the undertaker said solemnly,
relieved at the outcome of the emotional scene before
him. 'There's not a lot of men in these parts who own
dark suits, let alone wear them on days when it
promises to be as hot as this. You'll find you're dressed
as well as most of the men there.'

'Then that's OK.' Ryan smiled down at the girl he
was holding. 'Any more objections, Miss O'Meara?'

Rose looked up at him, dazed. To have him come with her? She had dreaded this morning with a fear that surpassed almost anything she had known before. It was true that she and her grandfather had kept themselves apart. They hadn't needed others, and for all of Rose's life she had been aware that the town disapproved of the reclusive old man and his wild, untamed granddaughter. They had used Rose when they needed her, but they disapproved nonetheless.

That disapproval didn't mean that the funeral would be small, though, she knew. Kora Bay turned out in force for funerals, and Rose knew that she faced a morning of easy sympathy and much more intense curiosity. To have someone beside her, to deflect the worst of the questions. . . Someone. . .

It was Ryan's presence she wanted, she acknowledged fairly to herself. To have Ryan beside her, driving away the worst of the isolation. . . To make her feel as if in her grief she wasn't absolutely alone. . .

She looked up at him and what she was feeling must have reflected in her face. She didn't have to say anything. Ryan knew what her answer was.

'Fine,' he said softly, and his twisted hand caught hers and held her tightly in its grip. 'Come on then, Dr O'Meara. Let's do what we have to do.'

His hand held hers all the morning. Ryan didn't release Rose's fingers once. He sat with her in the front pew while the priest talked simply about Tom O'Meara's long life.

Rose's tears had ceased. She listened with simple pride to what the priest had to say about her grandfather. It had been his time to die, she knew. She couldn't be sad for him. His heart condition had made him weaker and weaker, and with an aortic aneurism the end was inevitable. To regret his passing was selfish—an acknowledgement of loneliness—and while

Ryan Connell's fingers gripped hers in their strong clasp she wasn't alone.

Afterwards she stood in the graveyard and accepted the town-folk's sympathy with as much dignity and grace as she could muster. It was so much easier with Ryan. He answered many of the questions for her, intervening when he felt her hand tighten and knew that emotion was threatening to overwhelm her. The worst of the impertinences didn't happen. People looked at Ryan and their inquisitions about the state of Rose's finances or comments as to the future of O'Meara Cruises or Rose's medical career died on their lips.

There were many more unanswered questions being formed in their minds about Ryan Connell, Rose knew, but she didn't care. She let her hand lie in Ryan's clasp and felt nothing but gratitude for its comfort. Today she needed him desperately, and she had the honesty to acknowledge it.

In deference to tradition there was a light lunch served in the funeral parlour afterwards. Rose didn't eat a thing. She stood and tried to smile, answering questions, watching the town-folk eat what she was paying for and trying not to be bitter. Most of these people were here just out of curiosity. Or a free feed, she thought, trying to work out who some of those present were. She was sure she had never seen some of them in her life before.

Ryan still gripped her hand. As the luncheon dragged on she attempted a smile up at him. 'You don't have to stay,' she said feebly. 'I can manage.'

'Don't be a fool.' He tempered his harsh words with a smile and turned to field a question from an elderly matron by his side.

And finally, finally it was over. The last of the 'mourners' drifted away and Rose and Ryan were left alone. For the first time for hours Rose lifted her hand from Ryan's grasp. He released her and stood, looking questioningly down at her.

'What now, my Rose?'

Rose flushed. There was no mistaking the tenderness in his voice. The unshed tears of the morning threatened to return and she turned away swiftly.

'I'll go home,' she said quietly. 'I can walk to the cottage from here.' She took a deep breath and turned back to face him, determined not to cry. 'Thank you,' she said simply. 'You were. . . I. . . I needed you.'

Ryan looked down at her, his eyes expressionless. His mouth was tight and suddenly bitter. 'It's nice to be needed.' His voice was almost mocking. Then, as he saw her face change in confusion, he shook his head angrily and gripped her hands again. 'What are you doing this afternoon, Dr O'Meara? Running a cruise?'

Rose shook her head. 'I don't think I'm up to finding crocodiles today,' she said bleakly.

'Good,' he said decisively. 'We'll go out to the reef.'

Rose frowned. 'I'm sorry?'

'We'll go to the reef,' he repeated. 'I'm told it takes fifteen minutes to reach the Barrier Reef from here. Is that right?'

'I guess so.' Rose tried to make her mind think straight and only partially succeeded. 'In your boat, I guess.'

'Then let's go. We can be contacted by radio if we're needed.'

Rose shook her head. 'Dr Connell. . .'

'Ryan,' he said harshly.

Rose took a deep breath. 'Ryan, thank you for this morning,' she repeated. 'But you've done enough. You don't have to keep being kind.'

He shook his head. 'I've told you before,' he said firmly. 'I very seldom do things to be kind. I have all the charts for the reef but the locals tell me they can be treacherous and I'm better with a local pilot. Am I right in thinking you'd know the reefs around here like the back of your hand?'

Rose nodded uncertainly. She and her grandfather had spent many wonderful days exploring the magnificent coral reefs surrounding Kora Bay. 'Yes. But I don't. . .'

'Then we're set,' Ryan said firmly. 'No more arguments, Dr O'Meara. I've done you a favour this morning and now it's up to you to repay the favour. This afternoon you'll take me on a tour of the Great Barrier Reef. Agreed?'

'But. . .'

'Agreed?' he demanded again and Rose shook her head helplessly. She could no sooner deny this man than she could fly.

The *Mandala* reached the edge of the inner reef in les than the fifteen minutes Rose had promised. The huge cruiser cut through the mainland and the departing mourners far behind.

Ryan didn't need her. For all the man's talk of needing a pilot, with the charts by his side Ryan steered safely and surely through the treacherous reef waters, guiding his boat to the outer reef without any assistance from Rose. Rose was left to sit in one of the huge, canvas sun-loungers on the deck and soak up the sun.

The sun and the sea could always soothe her. Rose lay back and acknowledged that she needed this time away from Kora Bay. To go home to the empty cottage after such a morning would have driven her to the edge of despair.

But did she need to be with Ryan Connell? She looked over to where he stood behind the wheel, the sun on his ruffled brown hair and his back turned to her. He was intent on his course, his attention solely on the reefs surrounding the boat. His eyes were creased against the glint of sun on sea. He was a man at one with his environment.

Why had he done this for her? Ryan Connell didn't do things to be kind, he had told her, and yet this morning he had been kind. Rose couldn't have made it through such an ordeal without him. She thought of the events of the morning and how he had smoothed her dreadful task, and the anger and resentment she had been feeling faded to nothing. There was only gratitude.

Gratitude. . . Rose turned the word over in her mind, examining it from every side. Was that what she was feeling? She looked over at Ryan and knew that gratitude didn't describe her feeling towards Ryan Connell at all.

Gratitude. . . It wasn't close to what she was feeling. She watched as the breeze stirred through Ryan's hair. . .as he raised his damaged fingers to the wheel. . .as he looked down once more at his maps and then as he turned to smile at her. . .his deep, heart-wrenching smile that went straight to the core of warmth deep within her and slowly spread. . .

'According to my calculations we should be almost over Marley Reef,' he smiled. 'Am I right, please, miss?'

His words were meek but his tone was laughing, and Rose shook herself out of her numb lethargy and smiled back. He seemed to be making such an effort to be pleasant and in a corner of her mind she wondered why. It didn't matter, she told herself. She should just accept this day as a respite, before the rest of her life took over. Before the bills started pouring in and the search for crocodiles began again, and her repetitive spiels to the tourists and all those 'soon' imperatives. . .

She rose stiffly to her feet and crossed to the bench beside the wheel where Ryan had laid out the maps.

'We're here,' she told him quietly, pointing to a band of light blue on the map. 'We're at the northern tip of Marley. If you want to dive it's a good spot.' She hesitated. 'One of the smaller tour operators has a dive platform anchored not far from here. He doesn't run on Friday so if we wanted to tie to the platform. . .'

'Sounds great,' Ryan smiled. 'And yes, I do want to dive. Do you?'

Rose looked down ruefully at her serviceable clothes. To dive would be lovely—to slip into the warm, tropical water and lose herself in the magic of the coral garden below the boat. 'I should have brought my gear,' she told him. 'It doesn't matter. I'll sleep on the boat while you dive.'

'There's a chest full of swimming-gear in the cabin.' Ryan grinned. 'You'll have to find another excuse than that. Can you scuba dive?'

Rose nodded, frowning. 'I can. But. . .'

'Then no more arguments,' he said firmly. 'Now where is this platform?'

It was a magical afternoon. From the moment Rose slid her rubber-clad body into the crystal-clear waters above Marley Reef she felt as if she had been released from a slowly steaming pressure-cooker. The pain and the tension of the last few days—of the last few years— lifted like magic. The reef was magic. It could hold her in thrall like nothing else. Every time she dived it was as if she had been transported into a place of such beauty that she could hardly bear it.

And Ryan was with her. Rose had dived alone since her grandfather had become ill and had almost forgotten the pleasures of sliding through the water with someone beside her—someone to show the magnificence of the blue staghorn coral, the wide, gaping mouths of the giant clams, the flashing gold of the butterfly fish or the more subtle beauty of the tang, or the coral cod. Rose drifted lazily, letting the fish flash past her in colourful schools, occasionally stirring herself to take Ryan's hand and point out something of interest—something her grandfather had shown her and she had never shown another.

It was as if the reef was theirs and theirs alone. The world waited on the surface but down here she and Ryan were in a world apart. A giant manta ray drifted over their heads, its 'wings' lazily flapping, as unconcerned about the two human intruders in its territory as the humans were about it. A white-tipped shark came close behind and Rose looked a question across at Ryan. Did he know it was harmless? It seemed he did, or if he didn't he was unconcerned at the risk. Ryan seemed as content to drift and let the beauty of the place enthral them as was Rose.

As the air in their scuba tanks ran low they surfaced, and then shallow-dived, drifting on the surface with snorkels and masks. Rose wanted nothing more, and Ryan seemed to sense her need for this time apart. By drifting beath the water's surface they couldn't talk, and Rose didn't want to talk. She wanted nothing.

It wasn't completely true, she acknowledged to herself. After this morning, the sea and the coral would have been therapy for her frayed mind even if she had been alone, but Ryan's presence was a blessing. If she could have waved a magic wand and had him disappear—have the reef to herself—she wouldn't have done it, she acknowledged. With him she felt as if she wasn't completely alone in her life. It was an illusion, she knew, but it was an illusion she would hold on to for as long as she could.

Finally she had had enough. She pulled herself reluctantly out on to the diving platform and then lay in the sun, watching Ryan still drifting on the surface of the calm sea. The diving platform had an awning for shade. As the sun became too hot, Rose rolled lazily under cover. Her eyes closed and she slept.

She woke to find Ryan standing over her, fully dressed. He was carrying two large iced drinks, full of lemon and crushed shards of ice. Rose rolled over and looked up at him, his muscled frame clearly delineated against the sinking sun.

'Wha. . . What. . .' She put her hand to her eyes, confused.

'I'd let you sleep until morning,' Ryan smiled. 'But you're my pilot. And while I think I can navigate these reefs in daylight, I don't trust my luck at night.'

'Do you have a depth-sounder?' Rose asked.

'Mmm.' He handed her a drink and moved to sit in a deckchair bolted on to the platform under the awning. 'That's very handy for stopping me actually coming aground, but it doesn't stop me from getting hopelessly lost.'

Rose smiled. 'I can get you home from here,' she reassured him. 'I've done it hundreds of times.'

'With your grandfather?'

Rose's face clouded. 'With my grandfather.'

Ryan took a sip of his drink, his eyes on the smooth, sunlit water around the platform. 'You were lucky to have him,' he said gently.

Rose flashed a curious glance across at the man beside her. His scarred face looked grim, as though thinking of things he would rather not remember. For a moment he seemed even more alone than her, a powerful man, but one who had chosen a lonely road. Maybe there were different types of loneliness, she thought bleakly—the kind that was imposed on her by the deaths of first her parents and then her grand-father—or the exile that Ryan Connell had imposed on himself by his wealth and his decision to live a nomadic existence on his wonderful boat.

'Where's your secretary?' she asked suddenly. She hadn't seen any sign of Roy.

'When I have a holiday so does Roy,' Ryan told her. 'God knows, there aren't many of them. As of Monday we'll be putting our heads down and working solidly.'

'There aren't. . . You won't be terribly busy in Kora Bay,' Rose told him. 'Most of the patients go to Batarra.'

'Because they haven't thought you were qualified.'

'I'm not. . .'

'We'll talk about that later,' he said firmly. 'But for now. . . Well, I have plans for Kora Bay.'

'What sort of plans?' Rose asked curiously. She felt like a cat before a too warm fire—totally lethargic and lazily content.

'Kora Bay needs a hospital.'

'A hospital?' Rose's eyes widened. 'You can't. . .'

'Who says I can't?' he demanded lazily, taking a long sip of his drink. 'I thought you knew that I can do anything I want, Dr O'Meara.'

Rose raised her eyebrows and smiled reluctantly. 'And how do you intend to build a hospital?' she asked. 'I suppose you intend to have it open and running by Monday?'

'Well, not quite.' He grinned, a sleepy, humour-filled smile that did something strange to Rose's heart. 'Maybe by Tuesday.'

'Oh, yes?'

'There's a huge old house up on the headland overlooking the town.'

'The Bradshaw place.' Rose grimaced. 'It's been empty for years.'

'Not any more. I've builders starting on Monday, pulling the inside apart and readying it for patients.'

'But you can't. . .' Rose gaped at him. 'Have you thought? The work. . . The money. . . The regulations. . .'

'I told you, Dr O'Meara. I can do anything I want.'

'But it'll cost thousands. . .'

'I've spent the last two days costing. I have a rough idea how much it will cost and I'm going to do it.'

'And. . .and you'll keep practising from the *Mandala*?'

He shook his head. 'No. I'll use the *Mandala* for visiting patients on the coast, but she can go back to being mainly a pleasure-craft.'

Rose fell silent. There was, it seemed, nothing to

say. A hospital. . . It would be fantastic for Kora Bay. If only she had been able to do it. . .

'And speaking of plans for the future brings me to my next point,' Ryan went on. He was watching her as if he could read her mind. 'Roger Bain tells me there are at least four qualified nursing sisters in town, most of whom would love a job, and more in the district who might be tempted. I can't run a hospital, though, with only one doctor. I'd like you to take on a permanent position.'

Rose gasped. 'But. . . But I can't. . .'

'Why not?'

'You know why not.' Rose rose shakily to her feet. The warmth of the sun was doing strange things to her. Her head spun and she put a hand to the rail to steady herself. Before she reached it Ryan had risen and his hands held her.

'I don't know why not,' he said steadily. 'Suppose you tell me.'

'Because I'm not qualified.' She was close to tears. 'This. . . This isn't fair. It was. . .it's my dream to practise properly in Kora Bay, but now. . . I have to go to the city and do my residency. Maybe. . .maybe in twelve months if there's a vacancy. . .'

'No.' He held her sternly. 'Now, Dr O'Meara.'

'But I can't!' She practically yelled it at him.

'We're complementing personalities, Dr O'Meara,' Ryan mused. 'You say "I can't". I say "I can". And I'm right.'

'How can I?' she asked tearfully. 'I'd even get into deep trouble if the Medical Board finds out I performed an anaesthetic last night.'

He shook his head. 'That's just where you're wrong, Rose,' he told her seriously. 'I covered myself there. When I was at the Batarra hospital, settling Cathy, I had the opportunity to talk to Steve Prost, the GP who's been servicing Kora Bay. I also talked to the local surgeon. Both told me of the work you've been doing here—supposedly under their supervision—and both couldn't speak highly enough of you. They're willing—in fact they're eager——to speak to the Board about you, and we're ready to bet the two years' work you've done here will be accepted in lieu of your residency.'

Rose's eyes widened. She stared up at him. 'They'd do that?' she whispered. 'For me?'

'For you and for Kora Bay. Steve's fed up with travelling down here once a week and is delighted with my plans. They see also that Kora Bay will be losing a damned fine doctor if you leave—and they'll take the necessary steps to see that won't happen.'

Rose stared up at him, unbelievingly. Ryan's deep grey eyes looked calmly back. He was telling the truth. She could practise her medicine.

'You'll have to make a trip to Brisbane to front the board,' Ryan warned. 'But you won't be needed until we get the hospital. Jokes aside, it should take about six weeks to get the hospital up and running. We don't need two doctors while hospital cases still go to Batarra, so you can keep your crocodile-hunting up until then. When the hospital's ready we'll both go to Brisbane. I'll register the hospital and I'll support you while you register yourself. Now, Dr O'Meara, do you want this job I'm offering or don't you?'

Rose burst into tears.

She cried for a long time. Ryan held her until the worst of her emotion passed. The culmination of the events of the last few days found release in her tears, and Ryan Connell had enough sense to let her have her cry out. He held her gently, his arms softly stroking the curves of her back as the racking sobs slowly eased.

Finally, reluctantly it seemed, he put her away from him.

'Do I take it that means yes?' he asked, and Rose gave a watery chuckle.

'Yes,' she whispered.

He smiled down at her. 'That's great,' he told her softly. 'I couldn't ask for a better partner.'

'Partner. . .'

'Partner. I won't do it on any other basis.'

Rose frowned. 'But. . . But you'll be putting in all the capital. I. . . I have nothing. . .'

'We'll work out the fine-tuning later,' Ryan said firmly. 'It's Steve's day to visit Kora Bay and I asked him to keep doing it this week so we're covered. Today we don't talk work. It's rarely I allow myself a day off for pleasure.'

'So that's what this has been,' Rose said slowly. 'Taking me to my grandfather's funeral was pleasure?'

He looked down at her, his eyes following the slim lines of her bikini-clad figure. It was the most decent bathing-costume Rose had found in the chest of bathing-equipment the *Mandala* boasted, but it was hardly the most respectable thing Rose had ever worn. 'You could say there has been a fair element of pleasure for me in today,' Ryan said gravely, and Rose flushed.

'I'll. . . I'll go and get changed,' she said uncertainly. 'We should be getting back.'

'Do you have pressing engagements in Kora Bay tonight?' Ryan asked gently.

Rose shook her head. 'No. But. . .'

'Then we'll eat out here, if you can guide us back to Kora Bay after dark,' Ryan told her. 'I've prepared dinner while you slept.' And then as he saw her face change he smiled and shook his head. 'Not mud-crab,' he told her.

Rose gave a reluctant smile. 'I'm sorry.' She hesitated. 'I was. . . I was rude last night. . .'

'So make up for it tonight,' Ryan said firmly. He threw her a towel from the arm of the chair where he sat. 'I believe you know where the bathroom is, Dr O'Meara.'

Rose took a deep breath. 'I'm not having a bath, Dr Connell.'

'Ryan. We're partners. I refuse to be called Dr Connell by my partner.'

'I'm not having a bath, Ryan.'

He smiled and shrugged. 'Suit yourself, Rose.' His use of her first name was warmly intimate—a caress—as was the smile that followed the word. 'There's a shower near the bath. But I'd get the salt off, if I were you. My taste runs to sweet rather than savoury.' His smile deepened as he saw Rose's eyes widen and heard her indignant gasp. 'A joke, my Rose,' he said, his eyes laughing at her. 'Go and get yourself clean, or I'll have to take matters into my own hands.'

Rose went.

CHAPTER SIX

RYAN cooked steak and salad while Rose was showering. She emerged, once more clad in her serviceable clothes, to find him placing two laden plates on the table out on deck, and opening a bottle of wine.

'Just one glass each,' he smiled as he saw her look. 'We've still some reefs to negotiate tonight.'

'Thank you, but I won't have any wine,' Rose told him unsteadily. Wine was the last thing she needed. Wine and Ryan Connell's smile. . .

He shook his head. 'Now that's where you're wrong, Dr O'Meara. It seems to me that you haven't eaten a decent meal for days. Last night you left before I could bully you into eating. Tonight you have nowhere to run.' Once more he smiled down at her, his eyes compelling and warm. 'So you eat.'

'I don't. . .'

Again he shook his head, silencing her by placing a finger against her lips. He handed over a glass of chilled white wine and then raised his glass towards her. 'Not "I don't",' he said firmly. 'For tonight, the words are "I will".'

Rose looked up at him, her eyes confused. I will. Easy enough to say, but. . .

'All I'm ordering you to do is eat your steak and drink your wine,' Ryan said gently, seeing her confusion. 'I'm demanding nothing else.' He smiled. He grimaced ruefully, his burnt face twisting. 'Nothing.' He sat down before her and picked up his own wine. 'Now eat.'

To her surprise, Rose did manage to eat.

The beautifully marinaded and grilled steak slid down effortlessly, as did the salad. Then Ryan peeled sun-ripened mangoes for her, and served them with a rich, creamy ice-cream. The combination of the long swim this afternoon and her lack of appetite of the last few days made every mouthful taste like nectar.

Rose drank only one glass of wine, but that glass affected her. It must be the wine, she thought. Nothing else could spread such a glow of warmth and contentment through her on a day such as this. . . She had buried her grandfather but she had become a doctor again. With his self-sacrifice, her grandfather had educated her and made her a doctor, and now Ryan Connell, with a wave of his magic wand, was enabling her to practise.

Finally Ryan cleared the dishes and brought coffee out to the deck. They drank slowly, lulled into peace and silence by the sheer beauty of the setting sun over the sea. The boat rocked gently on the ocean swell, hardly enough to disturb them. Only enough to assure Rose that she was on her beloved ocean.

'We'd best be getting back,' Ryan said slowly, reluctantly it seemed to Rose. 'The working world waits. Steve will be gone by now. Though I did radio Roy and tell him to contact us if we were needed.'

Rose nodded just as reluctantly. Her fears had ebbed completely. For a while she had been afraid of this man, but that was light-years ago, she thought. She wasn't afraid he would take advantage of her now. She thought back to his grimace as he said he was demanding nothing. Ryan Connell was scarred, she thought, and not just physically. It was he who was saying they should return. If it were up to her. . .

What on earth was in that wine? she thought in stunned amazement as she realised where her thoughts were taking her. Her thoughts were drifting to places they had never been before and every thought was centred around Ryan Connell—Ryan Connell standing before her—Ryan Connell holding out his hands to help her to her feet. She placed her hands in his and a thrill went through and through her body at his touch. Those hands. . .

She didn't release his hands as she rose. She stood looking down at his larger hands clasping hers—at the damaged fingers. . .

'Ryan, how were you burned?' she said softly.

She heard his swift intake of breath and she felt a tug as he tried to withdraw his hands. She retained her clasp, her slim fingers entwining themselves in his.

'I'm sorry my burns offend you,' Ryan said stiffly, and Rose looked up at him in amazement.

'Offend me?' She shook her head. 'Ryan, your fingers don't offend me.' Then, as she saw the swift negation of his head-shake and realised he was rejecting her assurance, she tightened her grip on his injured hand. Slowly she bent her head and kissed it. 'Your fingers don't offend me,' she said softly. 'Nothing about you could offend me, Ryan Connell.'

For a long moment Ryan stood absolutely motionless, his dark, fathomless eyes watching Rose's still damp mass of chestnut hair falling over his hand. Then, as if fighting a war with himself and losing, he sighed and took her shoulders in his hands. He straightened her to face him.

'Rose. . . You don't know. . .'

'Tell me, then.'

He shook his head. 'I can't. Rose, I don't want. . . Rose. . .'

The word stretched out before them in one long sigh. It drifted out across the still water and back again, still echoing. 'Rose. . .' Whatever it was that Ryan Connell didn't want was drifting to nothing.

And then slowly, infinitely slowly, Ryan bent his head and kissed her.

Rose welcomed his lips with joy. She lifted her face to receive him, her lips hungry for him. She had wanted this, she knew. Last night. . . Last night's kiss had been a kiss of anger—a kiss of punishment and emotional turmoil—but it had lit a fire within her that refused to be quenched.

Her lips parted in welcome at the feel of his mouth, welcoming him into her. Her tongue tasted him and her hands came up to pull his head closer.

They stood, endlessly locked, the boat rocking slightly with the motion of the gentle swell, and the warm salt breeze caressing their entwined bodies like a blessing. The kiss was without beginning and without end. It was a living, breathing thing, breathing warmth and love into two new lovers.

Lovers. . . The word swept into Rose's mind and she let it drift as she moved her lips to take more of Ryan to her. That's what we are, she thought. For this moment we are lovers.

She had never been such a thing before. Lovers were star-struck teenagers—local girls with money and clothes to go to the Friday night dances, or ex-student friends who flirted and dated instead of keeping their heads in their books. Rose had thought they were foolish. Maybe they were, but then maybe they had never been kissed by Ryan Connell. . .

Ryan's hands were on her slim waist, pulling her body against his as his mouth held her to him. Rose could feel a raw desire in his body that matched her own and she gloried in it. She wanted him so much. And for this moment he wanted her.

For how long? Once again the errant thought flashed through her mind and once again the thought was irrelevant. Ryan Connell was promising nothing. 'I don't want. . .'

He didn't want her? He didn't want a woman?

Well, for now—for this moment—she needed him, and that had to be all that mattered. If he released her now she would go home tonight to her empty, desolate cottage. The thought was unbearable.

If he released her. . .

He had to, her head screamed suddenly. This man

was going to be a partner. A work associate. Somehow. . .somehow they had to build a working relationship and she was risking that in her need of him.

But for now. . . For now she was aching in a way she
had never ached before, and the thought of leaving
Ryan Connell and going home to her cottage was
unthinkable. There was a fire in her thighs she could
hardly believe. It wasn't Rose O'Meara who was
responding to this man. Once again a stranger had
taken over her body, a stranger with feelings and
desires she had never believed she could possess.

His hands were making her body move against the
rough fabric of his clothes. She lifted her hands to run
her fingers through his coarse hair and she let her body
move to the command of his hands. She could feel his
desire as she pressed her thighs against him and she
gloried in it. Her breathing was coming fast. His lips
released her and she flung her head back, her chestnut
curls cascading down her back and the smooth arch of
her neck exposed to his mouth.

He kissed her arched neck, his lips moving over the
smooth skin with a slow, sensuous appraisal. And then
suddenly she was thrust away.

'Rose. . .' Ryan's voice was thick with passion but
he cut through her aching need. 'Rose, do you want
this. . .?'

She sobbed his name, burying her mass of curls in
his shoulder. 'I want you,' she managed. 'Ryan. . .'

He took her shoulders and pushed her back. 'Rose,
listen. . .' He shook his head, as if trying to make
himself think. 'Rose, I can take precautions, but are
you sure you want this? I won't. . . I won't have you
saying I seduced you. . . Rose. . . Dear God, I swore
I'd never take another woman. . .'

Rose shook her head, her smile wiser than her years.
Caution was for another time. Her grandfather had
taught her to be free, and to react to her instincts.

Well, she was reacting now. This was her man. For now, Ryan Connell was hers.

'You're not taking me,' she whispered. 'I'm taking you, Ryan Connell. For now. . . For tonight I'm seducing you.'

He moved convulsively against her and then shook his head. He was having trouble finding his voice. 'Rose, I can make no promises,' he said hoarsely. 'I want no long-term commitment. I want. . .'

'All I want is this moment,' Rose told him. Her fingers moved, exulting in the reaction her touch was producing. 'I want you now, Ryan Connell. So much. . .'

He moved then, out of reach of her probing fingers. 'Are you sure, my Rose. . .?'

She nodded, suddenly solemn. 'I've never been so sure of anything in my life,' she said softly. 'This is right. For now, it's right.'

Ryan's face broke into a smile, a smile at once exultant and infinitely tender. He reached out and unfastened the buttons of her blouse, slowly, one by one, as if the act was one of reverence. Then he found the button and zip of her skirt. Both garments fell unheeded to the deck. He lifted her bra carefully over her head as Rose let her panties slide down. At last she was naked, free, and she had never felt so wonderful. She lifted her arms above her head and stretched, arching her back, tantalising the man before her.

She was free. . . The warm night breeze caressed the satin smoothness of her skin but she wanted more. Her body wanted more. . .

'I hated that outfit,' Ryan said huskily. 'All day I've hated those clothes. You can't believe the self-control I had to find when you put the damned things on again. They don't match the woman who wears them.' He placed a finger on her breast and gently teased the nipple. 'My Rose is wild and free. A wild and wondrous woman.' He shook his head. 'I've never met a woman as free as you. . . Or as beautiful. . .'

His hands moved from her breasts to enfold all of her, lifting her naked body to lie against him. He cradled her and he kissed her until Rose was close to sobbing with her joy. 'I couldn't want you more,' he said huskily. 'If I wanted you more I'd go crazy, you witch. More crazy than I am now. You beautiful seductress. . .'

Then, suddenly, she was being carried swiftly forward, not to the bathroom this time, but to the vast bedroom, with the big, waiting bed and soft sheets ready to receive her. . .

Rose's body responded in shock as she felt the soft linen. It was pure, animal pleasure she was feeling. She fell back, her hair cascading over the mounds of pillows. Her hands caught at Ryan as if to make him follow but he eluded her.

Rose's thighs were aching in need, but now she was forced to wait. She lay, drinking in the feel of the smooth, soft bedclothes against her skin as she watched Ryan's body emerge to nakedness before her eyes. Hours before, she had seen him in a bathing-costume and had known what effect his body had on her then, but this. . . He stood above her, and she had never seen a naked man in her life before but she knew that this was right.

She reached her hands up in supplication and he bent and gathered her into him. 'My Rose,' he said tenderly, his hands running the course of her nakedness, from the top of her still damp hair to her satin-smooth thighs. 'My Rose. . . My wild woman. . .'

Their naked bodies met, with such rapturous joy that Rose felt tears spring up behind her eyes. Skin against skin. . .her breasts yielding to the hard maleness of his naked chest. . .

'It has to be right,' she whispered to herself. Nothing could feel this good and not be right.

The moralists of Kora Bay would have a field-day if they could see her now, she knew, but then the moralists of Kora Bay had clucked over Rose since the day her parents had died. She was no lady, they had said. Well, she wasn't. She was taking this night for her own pleasure. She wanted Ryan Connell more than anything else on this earth. Her chances of having this man long-term might be non-existent, but tonight. . . Tonight he was hers.

And she was his. She belonged to him absolutely. There was no loneliness in her heart now. The desolation of the last few days was gone. There was only this moment. This body.

She moved closer. Closer. Her body gloried in his and she was closer to this man than she had ever thought she could be to any living person.

And then he moved and she found that there was a closeness she had not known existed. . . There was a closeness that could send her body into a blaze of glory that was beyond anything she could imagine. . .

'My Rose. . . My wild and glorious Rose. . .' He whispered the words, then suddenly he was moving down, down until she thought she would scream with joy and her world shattered on a crest of pain, and of joy, and of triumph.

He stilled. For a long, endless moment he stilled, and she could feel his shock. 'Rose. . .' His voice was suddenly unsure. 'Rose, is this your first. . .?'

'Don't stop,' she pleaded, her hands closing desperately on his body. 'Don't stop. . .'

He was past stopping. His hands moved again and although there was a new element of tenderness in his hold, the tenderness could not last. His need took over again. Rose's need took over.

The night shattered into a thousand shards of light as they became one, and then the shattered light suddenly came together into a flaming crescendo of fire.

As the fire slowly faded Rose knew that life for her had changed, and it had changed forever.

Rose woke to a sunlit, joyous dawn. She stirred as the first rays of the morning sun came through the windows of the boat to lie across the entwined lovers.

Rose didn't stir. 'Let me soak up this happiness,' she whispered to herself. 'Let me savour this warmth. . . this wonder. . .'

Ryan's arms held her even in sleep, his body cradling hers. She let herself drift in languorous pleasure. This was a tiny moment in her life, an episode that would soon be over. . .

Maybe she had been crazy. Maybe the night had destroyed her chances of working professionally with Ryan Connell. She tried to think dispassionately about him as she lay in his arms. Ryan Connell had money and a past life she knew nothing about. His burns only succeeded in making him more ruthlessly attractive. He had looks and charm and he could have any woman he wanted, she decided.

There was no future for Rose with Ryan Connell. She knew that as surely as she breathed. Ryan Connell was rich, sophisticated. . . He moved in a world apart from Rose's world. He had decided on a whim to set up a hospital in Kora Bay. If he stayed long enough to establish it before he moved on, then Kora Bay would be lucky. Rose would be lucky.

And Rose? Yesterday her future had been a life in a city she hated, and a job as a resident. Ryan Connell had given her back a future in Kora Bay, and she loved him for it.

Was that why she had given herself to him? She asked herself the question, trying to block out the lazy warmth of his arms as she lay considering.

Once, when she was still at school, a boy had asked Rose to the pictures. Afterwards he had taken Rose home. Her reception by the boy's parents had left them both stunned.

'There are plenty of decent women around without having to resort to the O'Meara girl,' the boy's mother had scolded, careless of Rose's presence. 'Look at her. She doesn't own a pair of shoes, or if she does I've never seen them. She spends her life up with that coarse-mouthed old man, learning Lord knows what, mucking about on boats. . . I want a daughter-in-law who can keep house—who can dress like a lady and who doesn't eat off her knife. . .'

'Mum, we're only fifteen,' the boy had protested weakly. 'I'm hardly likely to marry her. . .'

It had been enough for Rose. She had not protested that her grandfather had instilled manners into her from the time she could talk. She had turned and fled, and her tentative foray into Kora Bay's social life had ended then and there.

She didn't care. She hadn't enjoyed her first kiss, and until last night she had thought she must be frigid. Her grandfather's company had always been enough. She had been content to live her life alone, but now that her grandfather was gone it would be almost desolate.

But it wasn't desolate now. Not for this instant. . . this magical moment before the world took over. For now she could pretend that she was loved by a man called Ryan Connell—a man who she would give her life for if he asked it. . .

The thought flashed into her mind like a thunderbolt, and she gave an involuntary gasp. Was she in love with this man? She looked down at the hands clasped around her naked breasts and the sight of Ryan's scarred fingers wrenched at her heart. She knew nothing of him. Nothing. How could she be in love?

There was no how about it, her mind whispered grimly. It had happened without her knowing. As she had given her body to Ryan Connell, so she had given her heart. The transfer had been silent, painless and purely involuntary. It had been so easy. The pain would come later. . .

'I don't care,' she whispered defiantly to herself. 'There's nothing I can do about it anyway. I might as well take what comfort I can. . .' She shifted slightly, and Ryan's arms tightened.

'Going somewhere?' he said thickly.

Rose's bleak thoughts dissipated at the sound of his voice. For this moment there was only joy, and what joy! She turned within his clasp, twined her arms around her love, and kissed him deeply on the mouth. Then, with one swift movement, she pulled from his reach, out of the bed to stand against the open door. She stood, naked and lovely, laughing down at him.

'I need a swim,' she told him. 'It's only indolent city-folk who stay in bed on mornings like these.'

'Why, you. . .' Ryan made a lunge across the room at her but she was gone, running swiftly through the living quarters of the boat and out to the deck. Ryan reached the doors just in time to see the flash of her naked body as she dived straight down into the sea.

Rose had willed him to follow, but he didn't. Instead Ryan stopped at the rail. He stood on the deck, his eyes following the naked beauty of the lithe, lovely girl in the water below the boat.

She was disappointed, but would not let it show. Instead, Rose struck out for a coral cay, three hundred yards from the boat. It was submerged at high tide but now it lay exposed, its gleaming sands beckoning.

Ryan didn't follow. Rose reached the golden, glistening sands and stood, looking doubtfully back at the boat. Ryan had disappeared.

All of a sudden she felt stupid. This had been an impetuous action and she had been so sure he would follow. Now. . . Now there was nothing to do but to swim slowly back to the boat.

He met her at the diving platform. Ryan must have

showered swiftly. He was fully dressed. he bent over to help her from the water and silently handed her a towel. Self-consciously Rose wrapped it around her nakedness.

'We'd better be getting back to Kora Bay,' Ryan told her, and his voice was distant.

'Y. . . Yes.' Something had changed. His voice. . . His eyes. . . It was as if he had finally come to his senses. Rose stood looking up at him, her eyes waiting to be hurt.

'Damn.' Ryan swore violently and turned away. 'For God's sake, Rose, don't look at me like that.'

'I don't. . . I wasn't aware. . .'

'Like a dog waiting to be whipped.'

Rose clutched for her dignity, and anger came to her rescue. She pulled her towel tighter. 'I'll get dressed, then,' she said tightly.

He turned back to her then, and reached out. His hands held her shoulders for a long moment and then dropped away.

'Rose, what happened last night. . .'

'I know,' she said, in a thread of a voice. 'You regret it and it won't happen again.'

'Dear heaven, if I'd known it was your first time. . .'

'Then you wouldn't have touched me,' she whispered. 'But last night. . .last night I needed you.'

His eyes widened. 'Last night. . .'

'That was all it was, though,' she lied. 'Last night I was more alone than I've ever been in my life before, and. . .and what happened was what I wanted. You mustn't think. . .you mustn't think it means anything. . .that I gave myself to you.'

He frowned. 'I wish I could believe that.'

'It's true,' she lied again. She took a deep breath. 'Now. . . Now, if you'll excuse me I'll go and get dressed.'

He let her past. She had nearly reached the main doors when he spoke again.

'Rose. . .'

'Yes.' She stopped but didn't turn.

'Rose, from this moment we have to get our relationship on to purely professional terms.'

'I understand that.'

'I hope you do,' he said grimly. 'Rose, I'm not in the market for another relationship. . .another woman.'

Rose gasped. She turned back to him. 'Well, it's just as well you're not "in the market". Because I'm not for sale. And if you think you could have me just by lifting your little finger, you're very much mistaken, Ryan Connell. I have my own life and it doesn't include you. Now and forever.'

Now and forever. . . The phrase rang out in the stillness and Rose cringed. What she was saying was true. It had to be.

'Rose. . .'

'Let's leave it,' she said harshly. 'You're right. We have a professional relationship to consider and maybe last night was crazy. Consider it forgotten. And from here on, if you want to make love to someone then go back to your past life. If you aren't in the market for "another woman" then you'll just have to depend on your past. No matter. I'm sure that leaves you thousands to choose from. Now, if you've quite finished, I'm going to get dressed. And I'd ask you to get this boat moving. The sooner we're back in Kora Bay, the better I'll be pleased.'

CHAPTER SEVEN

THE *Mandala* berthed at her mooring at the estuary a little before eight.

Rose had sat in the bow of the big cruiser the whole way back, once more respectably clad in her hated, serviceable clothes.

This is where it ends, she told herself grimly, the euphoria of the night and the dawn fading as Kora Bay loomed on the horizon. This had been time out from her bleak world. She would go back now and face the empty cottage. . . But now. . . Now there was at least the thought that she could practise here as a doctor. There was a future for her here, thanks to Ryan. . .

Rose looked back to where Ryan stood behind the wheel. He, too, was now fully dressed and was gazing into the wind, his dark eyes still and contemplative.

Rose knew nothing of this man. She had feigned anger and uninterest and that was the way it had to stay. She knew nothing—only that she loved him.

He caught her look and smiled, but his smile was brief and distant. The night was receding.

Receding. Her love was receding. It had been a mad, crazy time that now had to be put firmly aside.

He had committed nothing of himself. He had shown Rose a side of herself she hadn't known existed, and for a while he had made her forget her sadness. He had given her back her career. She should be grateful. . .

Grateful. . . It was a word she couldn't apply to Ryan Connell. All Rose felt was love. . .

She was mad. Rose shook herself angrily, her hair flying in the breeze created by *Mandala's* swift passage.

How could she love someone of whom she knew nothing? How could she?

There was no answer in the gentle ocean breeze to her angry question. She only knew that she did.

For the next few weeks she could run her crocodile cruises and steer clear of the man. Maybe. . . Maybe by the time she came to work with him she would have come to her senses.

Ryan's secretary was standing on the jetty, waiting for his boss to return. Ryan must have radioed ahead. The middle-aged man smiled and waved a welcome and then caught the mooring-ropes Rose tossed across to be looped over the bollards.

'Thanks, Doctor,' he smiled, gentle eyes assessing Rose. 'That's my job you're doing.' He sprang on board as the *Mandala* settled back into its resting place and motioned down to where Rose's *Crocalook* swung against its mooring-ropes. 'The receptionist from the booking office came along about ten minutes ago to see if you were taking *Crocalook* out this morning,' he told Rose. 'Seems she's booked you a few passengers. And she says there's a queue in the first-aid room as well.'

Rose flushed, wondering what on earth this man must think about her. Roy's eyes were kindly and unassuming. Maybe Ryan Connell taught his secretary to react like this to all the women he entertained on board.

'If I've bookings then of course I'll be taking a cruise out,' Rose said quickly—too quickly. 'And I know I'm late for surgery.' She sounded defensive. She looked up at Ryan as he came towards her from the wheel. 'Thank you for. . .for the trip to the reef,' she said stiffly. 'I. . . I enjoyed myself.'

'I enjoyed myself too, Rose,' Ryan said softly, his eyes gently mocking. He looked down at her clothes and his brow twisted sardonically. 'Do you need a hand with surgery?'

'N. . . No. I can do it. You wanted until Monday off and. . .and I've kept you from your plans enough.'

'You have at that,' he said lazily, and grinned. 'Those clothes are nicely sensible for surgery but they haven't enough grease on for crocodile-hunting. I've a hire-car here. Can I drive you home?'

'No.' Rose held up a hand as if to fend him off. 'I don't need. . . I. . . I have clothes up in the first-aid room.'

He nodded gravely. 'Will you come to dinner on board tonight, then?' At her look he smiled and gave an almost imperceptible shake of his head. 'We have things to discuss, and Roy and I would welcome the company, wouldn't we, Roy?'

'We surely would.' Roy beamed, his eyes travelling slowly from his boss to Rose, and then back again. His grin deepened, as though he thoroughly approved what he was seeing. 'If we have company, I'm not expected to take dictation in between mouthfuls,' he told Rose. He fixed his boss with a glare. 'Setting up a hospital involves more paperwork than I've ever seen in my life.'

'That's why I value you.' Ryan grinned. He turned back to Rose. 'What about it?'

Rose shook her head slowly, avoiding his eyes. How could he not see what such an invitation would do to her? Somehow between now and the time they started working together she had to build herself some armour. She had no armour now. She was wide open to hurt. 'No,' she managed. 'I've. . .there's many things I have to attend to.'

'If there are problems then let me know,' Ryan told her firmly. 'I'm here to be used, Rose.'

Once again Rose nodded, but it was a defensive action that meant nothing. Here to be used. . . Like a friend and a workmate.

But she didn't want Ryan Connell as a friend or a workmate. She wanted him as her love, and to hope

for that was like wishing for the moon. 'Thank you
both.' She looked only at Roy. She couldn't look at
Ryan for the life of her. 'I'll remember that,' she said,
with as much dignity as she could muster. 'Thank you
again, Dr Connell, and goodbye.'

The first-aid room was packed when Rose finally
arrived. Rose groaned inwardly at the queue. Most of
the complaints were trivial though—things that could
easily have held off—and Rose finally realised that
most of her patients didn't want first aid. They wanted
a gossip.

Wasn't the new doctor handsome? Pity about the
burns, but it made him seem so much. . .well, so much
more interesting. Rose had obviously become friendly
fast, or had she known him before? What had caused
the burns? She didn't know! Goodness, and they
seemed such good friends.

Of course it was lovely that she had had him at her
grandpa's funeral. Her grandpa would have been
pleased to see her with such a nice young man. And
then he had taken her away straight after the funeral.
She'd been seen boarding the *Mandala*. And the
Mandala hadn't docked again until this morning.
Well. . .

By the time Rose finished she was furious. She was
almost tempted to get on a bus and head for Brisbane
anyway—away from the gossip-loving community. Her
last patient for the morning presented with a wound
that needed checking, and by the time Rose had
answered forty-seven questions she was just about
ready to clean the wound with straight iodine. Or
prescribe castor oil or a nice strong enema.

She finished later than usual, and then had to spend
time with Ray Leishman. Cathy's father was profuse in
his repentance and full of gratitude to Rose and Ryan.
Cathy was doing well, Rose was relieved to hear,

though she would have welcomed the news if Mr Leishman had been a bit less long-winded.

Rose ran late for her first crocodile cruise and then ran late all day. Her brain wasn't operating as fast as usual either. She found her thoughts drifting back and back to the night before. Luckily the estuary crocodiles were co-operative and her tourists were happy, chatting cheerfully among themselves and leaving Rose's thoughts free to wander where they would. They didn't wander. They stayed firmly on Ryan Connell.

The *Mandala* was deserted when she drew back to the marina for her lunch-break and to collect her afternoon's passengers. Rose was almost relieved. Somehow she had to get her life back to normal, keep to her routine and forget that yesterday had ever happened.

It wasn't possible, though. The sweetness of the night was too sharp—too poignant to leave her. It would stay with her forever.

The *Mandala* was still deserted when Rose tied up for the night. She ran her evening surgery, full of patients who were just as curious, if not more so, as the morning's lot, and then reluctantly started the long walk up the headland to her cottage. She hadn't been home since the funeral and her bicycle was still at home. She eyed the row of taxis outside the marina shops with longing. Rose was hot and weary. The last thing she wanted was a long walk, but a taxi cost money she could ill afford. If she could sell the business. . . She'd find time tomorrow to see the agent, she decided.

The little cottage seemed even more overgrown than usual as she trudged up the path. No Pa. . . Rose's mind was black with weariness and depression. There was no Pa to welcome her home with a hug and a demand to know all about her day. There was no one. She opened her door and a pile of envelopes lay waiting for her on the mat. She picked them up with reluctance, noting the many clear-windowed envelopes denoting bills, and walked through into the deserted kitchen. The silence was all-enveloping. Pa's absence was everywhere.

The bills could wait. Rose made herself a toasted sandwich, telling herself severely that she had to eat. She was too thin already. She made coffee and then picked up the pile of mail, taking it out on to the veranda to read.

It was weird sitting out here without Pa. It seemed almost wrong—as though she had no right to be here— as though life for everyone else should somehow stop with Pa's death. Rose made herself sit in Pa's wicker chair, knowing that she loved it. If she could overcome the reluctance to use it, then the chair could become a friend. A friend. . . She turned the word over in her mind as she started reading the pile of mail. She had so few friends. Had she any?

She opened the next envelope and took a sip of coffee, and then her hand stopped as she lifted the mug to her mouth for the second time.

Dear Miss O'Meara,

As you are aware, the policy of Kora Bay Marina Management is to discourage small tour operators from the marina. Because of community pressure, however, established operators such as your grand-father have been permitted to stay.

The contract to allow your operation to continue has been in your grandfather's name, and in his name only. Because of the policy regarding small tour operators, new contracts are not planned.

Therefore please accept this cheque, being a refund of all mooring fees for the unexpired period of your grandfather's contract. We would ask that O'Meara Croc Cruises cease operation forthwith.

Please also note that due to the commencement of

practice by Dr Ryan Connell, your employment as first-aid officer is terminated as of Monday next.

Please accept Marina Management's condolences on your grandfather's death.

Yours sincerely.

Roger Bain.

Rose didn't move. For maybe ten minutes she sat, looking down at the piece of paper in her hand, while her mug of coffee grew cold in her hand.

At one stage she half rose, with the intention of finding her grandfather's contract, but she let her shocked body fall back into the chair before she reached her feet. It was true that the contract to allow her crocodile cruise to operate from the marina had been in her grandfather's name. She had queried it once, just after she came back to Kora Bay, but she had been told by Roger Bain that she couldn't change the contract to include her name. At the time it had worried her, but as other worries crowded in she had forgotten.

So. . .

So O'Meara Crocodile Cruises was finished. She could sell the boat, maybe, but not as a business. She was under few illusions as to what the boat alone would bring—if it sold. She stared down at her cheque. It seemed ridiculously small for a sum that would have to keep her until she was employed.

'I need a job now,' she whispered. 'Not. . . Not at some future time when the hospital will be ready. Ryan says six weeks. . .'

Six weeks. There would be mountains of red tape. Six weeks was the absolute minimum. It would probably be more. Rose thought of the massive job to turn the derelict shell Ryan had purchased into a hospital and her head told her six months minimum. There were all the funeral bills to pay. And she had to keep the cottage if she was to stay here. . .

She looked down at the now crumpled letter in her hand. 'Cease operation forthwith. . .' She had been lucky Roger had allowed her to run her cruise today, she knew. Tomorrow was Sunday—her busiest day—and Rose just knew what he had in mind. It would give Roger Bain pleasure to have security tow *Crocalook* away from her moorings, embarrassing her before a boat-load of paying passengers.

She wouldn't give him the pleasure.

There was an old jetty around the bluff from the marina. It was ramshackle and decrepit now, used only by the local amateur fishermen, but Rose could take *Crocalook* and tie her there before Roger and his security people took control. She could do it tonight. At least that would save her embarrassment in the morning.

And then what? How was she going to live?

Maybe she should talk to Ryan. . .

'There's nothing Ryan can do about this,' she whispered. 'Apart from charity, and I'm damned if I'll accept charity from Ryan Connell.'

She stared at the miserly refund cheque in her hand. It wouldn't cover the funeral costs. If she didn't work. . . To have no money coming in. . .

She had never felt so lonely in her life. There was only Ryan. . .and that left no one at all.

'You couldn't ask,' she told herself harshly.

Maybe it would be better if she just left—left here and went down to Brisbane. It was October and the new residencies were starting now. Maybe. . . Maybe she'd be lucky and get work straight away.

She turned and walked across the veranda towards the door back into the cottage. There was nothing else to say. There was no argument to be answered. There was only her boat to be moved.

She knew she should feel something but she felt nothing, nothing at all. For a moment today she had let herself believe a dream, and now. . . Now there was nothing.

By the time Rose bicycled back down to the marina it was close to dark. The open air cafés on the esplanade were crowded with noisy contented tourists, settling in to their extended evening meal.

It was a perfect night for holidays. The moon was almost full and the breeze had dropped to nothing as night fell. Indoors it would be hot and stuffy without a breeze to move the warm air through the house, but outside it was magic, a balmy, moonlit night full of the scent of the sea and the perfume of the frangipani trees lining the road to the marina. The spent flowers were drifting down as she passed.

Normally Rose would have lifted her head as she rode and drunk in the scents and the feel of the tropical night. Not now. Now that it was lost to her, she wanted no part of it.

I wish I could leave tomorrow, she thought bleakly. Get out of this town now. The thought of tomorrow's inevitable interview with the bank manager, the estate agent and the boat-dealer left her cold.

The *Mandala* was in darkness, and for that at least Rose breathed a sigh of relief. She couldn't tell Ryan Connell what had happened. No doubt Roger would answer any enquiries Ryan might have when he found *Crocalook* was gone. Would he make enquiries? Rose wondered. Did he care enough to want to know?

Of course he would, Rose acknowledged as she lifted her advertising billboard from the jetty and carted it down on to the deck of *Crocalook*. He had offered her a job. But how much of that offer had been caused by sympathy?

'He'll probably be relieved I'm gone,' she told herself bitterly. 'He wanted me. . . It doesn't matter,' she responded again to herself, and her voice was even more bleak. 'It doesn't matter any more.' She stowed the billboard flat on *Crocalook's* deck, then climbed up on to the jetty again to bring her bicycle down. It was a long walk from here to the old jetty. The bike could come with her.

'Planning a midnight bike ride on a coral cay?' a voice asked quietly, and Rose jumped about a foot. She looked up and Ryan Connell was standing on the *Mandala* in the dark, looking down to where she stood on the jetty. She couldn't see anything but his silhouette against the moonlit sky but she knew it was Ryan. She could never forget that voice. She could never forget anything about this man.

Rose stood staring up stupidly for a full minute or even more, willing words to come into her head, but they refused to come. Finally she simply shook her head, lifted her bike and hauled it across and down on to her boat.

For a moment she thought he would make no other comment. There was silence. She didn't look again, but bent over *Crocalook's* engine in readiness to start her. To her anger when she lifted her hand to fit the key into the starter motor, her fingers were trembling so much she dropped the key. She bent to retrieve it from where it had fallen but Ryan was before her. His hand reached down and lifted the key into his grasp. As she turned to face him, he held the key up before her.

'Is this one of the "many things" you had to attend to tonight?' Ryan asked sardonically. 'A moonlight cruise with your bicycle for company?'

Rose flushed and held out her hand for the key. 'Yes,' she managed. 'Give me my key, please.'

He stood staring at her in the moonlight, his twisted brow making him seem angry. Maybe he was. . .'Why the bicycle?' he asked at last.

'It's none of your business,' Rose said desperately. The tears which had held back all night now threatened. 'Please, Dr Connell. . .'

'What the. . .?' Ryan moved suddenly, his hands coming forward to grip Rose's shoulders. 'What's wrong, my Rose?'

'I'm not. . .' Rose pulled back unsuccessfully in his hold. 'I'm not your Rose. We. . . Please. . . I'm busy. I have to. . .'

'What do you have to do?'

'It has nothing to do with you.' The tears slipped over now and Rose was powerless to stop them. Her feeling of helplessness was threatening to overwhelm her. 'Look, Dr Connell, you've been very kind but. . .'

'Kind, hell!' he said savagely, and his hands tightened on her until they hurt. 'Kind has nothing to do with it. I told you before, Rose O'Meara, that I don't do things to be kind.'

'Well, why do you do them?' she snapped, her fragile hold on control disintegrating. 'Why are you nice to me? If you're not helping me to be kind, then I can only assume you're playing some stupid, cruel game. And I don't want it any more, Ryan Connell. I. . . I thought. . . Last night was only because I was so. . .so lonely. Do you think you would have got near me if I hadn't been distraught? Or is that how you pick up all the virgins you seduce, Ryan Connell?'

The silence stretched out so long that Rose came near to collapsing. Her legs were having trouble holding her. She put her hand on the tiller to steady herself but it didn't seem to help.

She could hardly see Ryan through her tears in the dim light but she could feel anger emanating from him in waves. It struck her almost as a physical blow. She felt physically sick. In desperation, she made a grab for the keys in his hand. He allowed her to lift them from his grasp as she turned, shoved the key into the motor and the engine roared into life.

'I'm going,' she yelled, over the noise of the engine. 'If you have anything to say to me then say it, and get off my boat, Ryan Connell.'

'You little. . .' Ryan seized her and pulled her back to face him but Rose held on to the tiller for dear life. She longed to roar off into the darkened estuary but not with Ryan Connell standing beside her or with the ropes still tying *Crocalook* firmly to the bollards.

The ropes. . . She had to undo the ropes and that would get her away from this angry man. . .give her some leeway. . . With an almost superhuman effort she wrenched herself from his grasp and leaped up the ramp to the jetty. Ryan Connell stayed exactly where he was.

'Get off my boat,' Rose yelled again savagely. She took a deep breath. Here, up on the jetty and yards away from Ryan's angry presence, she could find some sort of control. She took a deep breath. 'Dr Connell, I am grateful to you for yesterday, but that's over. I've thought of your very kind job offer and I've decided to decline. End of interlude. Now, if you could leave me alone. . .'

'You don't want to be left alone,' Ryan said, his voice hardly rising but his tone cutting across the noise of the motor for all that. 'You wanted me last night. . .'

'Stop it!' Rose flung her hands up to her ears. 'Stop it this minute. If I let you make love to me last night it was because. . .'

She got no further. As she spoke she noticed for the first time that she and Ryan had an audience. A group of tourists had left the esplanade cafés and had wandered down to walk along the jetty. Rose took a deep breath. 'This is a private jetty,' she snapped.

'I can see why you'd want it to be.' An elderly tourist beamed at her from his vantage point underneath the jetty light. 'Don't mind us, dear.' He turned and took his wife's hand in his and then beamed back at Rose. 'The wife and I have three grown-up daughters of our own. We're quite used to lovers' spats. Emily here was just saying it made her feel almost as though we were back home to listen to you and your beau. . .'

Rose flushed bright crimson. She stared desperately at the group of tourists but they didn't budge. Finally she turned back to Ryan. 'You're making me a public spectacle,' she said bleakly. 'Please get off my boat.'

'I'm making you. . .' Ryan looked up at her and shook his head. 'It's not me who's hysterical and overwrought.'

'Get off my boat!' Rose was almost screaming with inner emotion. 'Get off my boat, Ryan Connell.'

'You know, I would, young man,' the elderly tourist advised Ryan. 'Seems your young lady's like to suffer a palsy stroke if you don't.'

'She's the first-aid officer here,' one of them announced in satisfaction. 'And he's the new doctor. Don't they make a nice pair?'

Ryan flashed a look up at the group of tourists and to Rose's fury she saw him grin. He lifted his shoulders in the age-old way of one man expressing to another his incomprehension of the ways of woman. Then he lightly sprang up to join Rose on the wharf. Crossing over to her, he lifted the heavy mooring-rope from her grasp.

'Get on your boat, Miss O'Meara,' he said firmly.

'But. . .'

'Oh, for heaven's sake, can we just cut out the histrionics?' Ryan said wearily. 'Get on your boat, take yourself off for your midnight bicycle ride, and we'll have this out when you return.'

'There's nothing to have out,' Rose whispered.

'Get on the boat,' he said again. 'I'll release the stern rope.'

For a long moment Rose stood looking up at him. She need never see him again, she knew. She would leave this mooring tonight and Ryan Connell would be nothing but a bitter-sweet memory. Involuntarily she put out her hand as if in sudden supplication, and then, as she realised what she was doing, she let it fall uselessly to her side.

'Thank you,' she whispered. She put a hand to her eyes to stop the sudden gush of tears, and then she turned and boarded her boat.

CHAPTER SEVEN

ROSE did a brief surgery the following morning. Sunday was always quiet. People were too busy on weekends to be ill, and even the desire to gossip about Rose and the new doctor wasn't enough to drive them to the first-aid room.

Tomorrow Ryan would take over. He had better facilities on the *Mandala* than Rose had now, and when he built his new clinic. . . Well, Rose certainly wouldn't be missed.

Even Ryan didn't need her. It would be easy enough for him to attract another doctor once Kora Bay had a hospital. Kora Bay would grow quickly. It was only its lack of medical facilities that had been holding it back now the marina was built, and Roger Bain would soon see that the new amenities were widely publicised.

Kora Bay. . . Rose couldn't think of Kora Bay. Not of its future—a future without her.

With her cruise cancelled, Rose was free to spend most of the day with her bank manager, her lawyer and the estate agent. It was fortunate Kora Bay was classified as a tourist destination, allowing local businesses to open at weekends.

She moved from one to the other with relentless energy, willing herself to get this ordeal over. She wanted everything settled. Every moment she had to spend in Kora Bay meant further heartache.

Her attachment to Kora Bay wasn't the main reason for her relentless haste, she acknowledged to herself. She also wanted to get as far from Ryan Connell as possible. She was no longer in control when he was around and she knew it. He brought out a side of her she hadn't known existed.

115

She had reacted to him with unreasonable anger last
night on the jetty. She had been rude and offensive,
but she knew no other way to drive him away. And she
had to drive him away. If she stayed near him
longer. . . His hope for a professional relationship was
crazy. If she fell any deeper in love. . .

Was it possible to be any further in love than she
was now? she asked herself bleakly. Surely not. She
shook her head as she walked down Kora Bay's main
street from the bank down to the lawyer's office. She
was like a schoolgirl suffering her first crush. This was
all her feeling for Ryan Connell was, she told herself.
A stupid, stupid crush. She had never met anyone like
Ryan Connell before and she was blinded by his sheer
animal magnetism. She knew nothing about him apart
from the fact that he was a skilled doctor. Nothing!

'He's probably got three wives and a woman in every
port,' she said out loud, causing a woman shopper she
was passing to turn and stare. It didn't matter. The
woman probably thought Rose was crazy, Rose
thought bitterly, but they all did in this damned town.
They now had their way, Rose acknowledged as she
trudged on down the main street. The respectable
matrons of Kora Bay had won. The O'Mearas were
finally finished.

By the time Rose reached her cottage that night she
had done almost everything that had to be done. The
lawyer was in control of the sale of *Crocalook* and the
cottage. He had power of attorney to make decisions
on Rose's behalf. She had paid one of the fishermen to
keep an eye on *Crocalook* until the boat was sold, and
she'd organised someone to tend the cottage's garden.
She had locked her first-aid room on the marina and
handed in the keys. There was nothing left for her to
do but to pack and catch the bus for Brisbane.

Pack. . . Rose wandered around her cottage and
wondered where on earth to start. This cottage held

her past. She went through into her beloved back bedroom. Here were the whale bones she'd dragged all the way up the headland after storms lashed the coast when she was a child. She remembered one in particular had taken her from dawn until after dark. 'If you want it then you bring it home,' her grandfather had growled, not realising the extent of his small granddaughter's determination. That night he had returned from his cruise to find one weary little girl proudly asleep under a canopy of a huge and still rather smelly whale bone.

And now? One of the local cafés would buy her whale bones, Rose knew, and the thought gave her no pleasure at all. Wearily she dragged her suitcase from the top of her wardrobe, and then froze as a knock resounded through the cottage.

'It'll be the boy who's going to do the garden,' she told herself firmly, recovering her equilibrium. The lad had promised to come round and see what had to be done. Still, it was a huge physical effort to walk through the cottage and open the front door. When she saw who it was it required an even greater physical effort not to slam the door closed again. Ryan Connell. . .

'Finished packing?' he asked pleasantly.

Rose gave an audible gasp. She leaned back against the doorframe as though she needed its support. 'I don't know. . . What do you mean?' she managed.

'Finished packing for Brisbane?' he repeated. 'I assume that's where you're going?'

'I. . . Yes.' Rose was almost gaping up at him. 'How. . .? How did you know?'

He raised his eyebrows uninterestedly. 'When your boat didn't come in last night I was concerned.' At Rose's look of incredulity he held up his hand as if to prevent her interrupting. 'Then I thought of the bicycle. You didn't take a bicycle without some purpose. So I drove the car around the inlet and discovered

Crocalook tied to the old jetty. It didn't take much deduction to figure out that Roger Bain was mixed up in your sudden departure. So I took myself in to see him this morning. . .'

'Roger Bain doesn't know I'm going to Brisbane.'

'No.' Ignoring Rose's involuntary movement of protest, Ryan walked past her into the cottage. He walked through into the kitchen and stood looking round. 'He told me what I needed to know though. He's just put you out of work.' He looked out of the windows to the ocean view beyond and whistled appreciatively. 'Great little place,' he approved.

Rose was left to follow the man into her own home. The anger which built as some sort of instinctive protection welled up within her.

'I didn't invite you in,' she said through clenched teeth. 'Will you please leave?'

Ryan shook his head. 'No,' he said again. He turned to face her. 'Rose, do you know what you're up against in Brisbane?'

Rose stared, her protective barrier slipping a little. 'What. . .what do you mean?' she stammered. 'I should think I can get a job without too much. . .'

'As a resident?' Ryan's brow came down harshly over his eyes, his scarred brow distorting further. 'If you think you can just walk into a hospital. . .'

'I'll get a casual job until I can,' Rose snapped. 'There's nothing here for me.'

'There's a medical career here.'

'In six weeks. Or six months, more likely. . .'

'Cut the nonsense, Rose,' Ryan said savagely. He reached forward and grabbed her wrist. 'Tell me what the hell is going on.'

Rose wrenched her wrist back but Ryan's hand held hers in a grip of iron. He hurt. She wrenched again, and his hold only tightened. 'There's nothing to tell,' Rose said weakly. 'You know I'm going to Brisbane and of course I have to get a job. Why else do you

think I'd go there? No one here will employ me. I
haven't a choice.'

'How broke are you?'

Rose shook her head. 'That's none of your business.'

'You tell me or I'll go through this cottage with a
fine-tooth comb until I find out.'

Rose glared up at him but his eyes were implacable.
He was quite capable of such an action. Her pathetic
bank-book lay on the table in front of her. She stared
down at it and Ryan's eyes followed her gaze.

'Tell me, Rose,' he said quietly.

'The bank manager has advanced me two hundred
dollars and agreed not to foreclose on the cottage for
three months,' she said bitterly. 'They'll cover my debts
until then. The cottage will be sold, though. It has to
be.'

'As broke as that?'

'My grandfather needed nursing,' she said simply.

'You could have put him in a nursing-home.'

'No.'

He stared at her for a long moment and his expres-
sive mouth twisted. 'Well, then,' he said finally. 'So
what are you going to do?'

'I'm going to Brisbane.'

He shook his head. 'Not yet. You'll starve. Two
hundred dollars will hardly pay the bus fare and a
couple of nights' accommodation.'

'But. . .'

'I know,' he said wearily. 'You have to work. So
you'll work. But here.'

'Look. . .'

He held up a hand. 'I'm not offering charity.' He
sighed ruefully. 'And I'm not offering this as an apol-
ogy for what happened last night—though God knows
I'm sorry. I think we were both crazy. The last thing I
want is entanglement with a woman, Rose. You have
to accept that.'

'I accept it,' she said stiffly. 'I told you. I know I was crazy.'

'And I took advantage of your emotions.' He dug his hands in his pockets. It was as if they were two strangers who didn't trust each other. Rose found she was shivering.

'I want you to get the hospital ready,' he told her.

'I. . .'

'Oh, for God's sake, Rose, shut up and listen,' he said wearily. 'And put your bloody pride some place where it doesn't get in the way of your sense. I saw Roger Bain this morning and he told me what he'd done. I told him a thing or two as well, which didn't make him too happy, but that's beside the point. It seems I have a medical practice to organise and a hospital to build from scratch. The sooner the hospital is running then the sooner the practice here will thrive. So. . . So I employ you to set up the hospital while I cover the medicine.'

'But. . .'

'I told you,' he said savagely. 'Shut up and listen. I'm assuming you're capable of organising the setting up of a hospital. It will mean you have to do the groundwork—travelling to Batarra and other centres to see how they're set up. You'd also have to find and employ nursing staff. Roy's overworked already, and seeing you know the locals, you're far better equipped for the job.'

'You. . . You'd employ me?'

'Yes. Our partnership would come into effect once the medical practice becomes viable for two. This is not charity I'm offering, Dr O'Meara, but a sensible business deal. Now, all you have to do is say yes.'

Rose stared up at him. This was crazy, her heart was saying, but her head was telling her it was sensible. She could set up the hospital—and she'd love doing it.

And Ryan was right. This wasn't charity. As soon as Ryan opened his surgery on Monday morning he'd have every curious local with complaints from ingrown toenails to sleeplessness coming to check out the new doctor. The locals knew he had excellent qualifications. They wouldn't go to Batarra—in fact she wouldn't be surprised if he found some Batarra residents coming here. He'd be busy enough to need her.

She could do it. And she could stay.

And hope. Could she hope that whatever spark had ignited within Ryan Connell would reappear? That the bitterness could be overcome?

You're being stupid, she told herself helplessly for the hundredth time. To stay. . .

But to leave was impossible. Not while there was that tiny, crazy hope.

'Of. . .of course I'll accept,' she said quietly. 'I. . . thank you.'

'Don't thank me yet,' he said harshly. 'You're going to work harder in the next few weeks than you've ever worked before.'

She did too, and she loved it.

The next few weeks saw Ryan Connell's dream become reality, and Rose was the driving force behind the transformation.

The rambling house set high on the headland looking out over town and ocean was the perfect setting for a hospital. Every room had views that would encourage the most dangerously ill patient to feel better.

That was all it had, though. The rooms were bare and forlorn, with aged wallpaper hanging in tatters, and mildew from the sea-air rotting into the plaster. Ryan Connell had brought a shell and it was up to Rose to transform it.

The structural part was easy. Kora Bay was a depressed community and tradesmen were easy to find, especially when Ryan Connell's wallet was so obliging. Rose saw how much this was costing and silently wondered. For the first couple of days she referred all

cost decisions back to Ryan but on her fourth phone
call for one afternoon he put a stop to it.

'I don't care how much the damned sterilisation unit
costs,' he snapped. 'I'm employing you to make sure
I'm not wasting money. Now, stop wasting my time.'

So Rose had gone back to her catalogues and chosen
a quality unit. It wasn't the cheapest, but it was good.

There was so much. Each of the rooms had to be
fitted with hospital beds, lockers, carpets. . . The list
was endless, and then there was the resuscitation
equipment for every room. Rose didn't ask Ryan about
that. If each room didn't have resuscitation equipment
then it was a nursing-home—not a hospital—and if
Ryan Connell was giving a hospital to this place then it
would be a good one. She ordered, looked at the cost
and winced, and then sealed the order.

Within two weeks she had the major structural
alterations complete. Then the massive fitting-out
began. Rose drove herself mercilessly. She hardly saw
Ryan. If they needed to communicate they did it
through Roy, a role Roy seemed to find amusing.

'You're like two pups with one bone,' he grinned at
Rose one night. 'Doc Connell's itching to be doing this.
It's nearly killing him to be seeing patient after patient
while this is going on.'

'Well, why doesn't he come and see?' Rose queried.
'He's hardly been near the place.'

'Cos he's given the bone to you,' Roy smiled.
'Doesn't stop him being jealous, though.'

Rose shook her head as Roy bade her goodnight and
left. It was fun. To build the hospital she would work
in as she wanted it. . .

As Ryan would want it too. She was intensely aware
of him as she made each decision. If she messed up. . .

She sighed and picked up some plans from the newly
carpeted office floor. Tonight the circus was playing at
Batarra and most of Kora Bay's population had headed
north. Roy had decided to go too. Not Rose, though.

She took the plans into the bare little room that would serve as Theatre and knelt on the floor to study them. The lights had to be decided on by tomorrow. She had to plan where the table would be. . .

'I'm not paying you overtime.'

Rose jumped about a foot. When she landed again Ryan Connell was standing over her.

'Good grief,' she said breathlessly. 'You scared the living daylights out of me.'

'You should lock the doors if you're staying late. I thought you'd be at the circus.'

Rose picked up her plans. 'I want to get this finished,' she told him, her mind racing. He had come tonight because he had thought she wouldn't be here.

He didn't seem perturbed by her presence now. Ryan stood looking quizzically down at her.

'Forgotten to order chairs, Dr O'Meara?'

'I have thirty-seven chairs ordered,' Rose told him stiffly. 'Two for every room, some for the sunroom, and office chairs for Sister's station. Oh, and kitchen chairs. They should arrive the day after tomorrow.'

'So meanwhile you sit on bare linoleum.' He grimaced. 'This is not exactly the work you've been trained for.'

'I love it.' Rose looked up at him and smiled shyly. For the first time a part of her carefully built up reserve slipped away. 'And it beats crocodile-hunting.'

'Honestly. . .'

'Honestly. To be doing this. . . Building a hospital from the ground up. Well, it seems. . .it seems almost a privilege.'

'I'm glad.' He smiled down at her, but his smile was strained. Rose gathered her plans and rose.

'I'm going to have the wiring done for the operating lights tomorrow and I need to figure out where the table goes,' she told him.

'Show me.'

Rose handed over the drawings, looking directly at

him for the first time. His eyes looked strained and the creases around the scar on his brow more deeply etched than usual. 'You look tired,' she said quietly.

'I am.' He grimaced. 'I don't know how the hell you practised here and ran the cruises.'

'Well, I didn't,' she told him. 'The locals knew I wasn't properly qualified. They usually went to Batarra. I only saw the minor work and emergencies. You're getting the lot.'

'And some,' Ryan groaned. 'I had a car-load of Batarra people in this afternoon with everything from earache to early pregnancy.'

'Coming to check the new doctor.' Rose smiled. 'You should have expected that.'

'Just as long as they go back to Batarra from now on.'

'It's a far cry from a physician's job in the city,' Rose offered.

'Yes.' Ryan's reply was curt. That other life was a closed book. He stared down at the plans in his hands. 'The operating table goes here?'

'Yes.'

'There's natural light to the left, though,' he offered. 'The table would be better slightly to the left and the sink here. Move it.'

'Yes, sir.'

He looked sharply across at her and then sighed. 'I'm sorry, Rose. I'm just. . .'

'Just tired?'

'Yes.'

She nodded, wishing she could help. If she could only offer to do night calls occasionally. . . Since the locals had learned there was a true medical service operating, Ryan had been called at all hours and it was showing. If they weren't careful, Kora Bay would have Ryan leaving before the hospital was even finished.

'We've got to get your registration through,' Ryan said grimly, as though reading her thoughts.

'Yes.'

'Should another two weeks have this place ready?'

Two weeks. Rose looked around and nodded slowly. She would never have thought it possible but the work that had been achieved already was little short of miraculous. 'I think so.'

'Do it,' he said curtly. 'I'll advertise for a locum for a few days and we'll do all our paperwork together.'

Rose drew in her breath. To go down to Brisbane with Ryan Connell. . .

'Look, I don't think so. . .'

'Don't think,' Ryan snapped wearily. 'Just do it.'

Their newly installed telephone rang as he turned to go. Ryan sighed and picked the instrument up from where it still lay on the floor. There was no desk yet to put it on. 'Kora Bay Hospital,' he snapped efficiently, and Rose blinked. It sounded almost as if it really was an operating, efficient little hospital.

Ryan was frowning into the telephone. 'How long?'

The temptation to listen was irresistible. Rose stood quietly, waiting, trying to piece together the full conversation from what she was hearing.

'Twenty-four hours!' Ryan's words were an explosion of incredulity. 'And you haven't contacted anyone? Have you got a midwife? No one!'

Rose saw Ryan's fingers clench on the phone. His face was a mixture of disbelief and dismay.

'Right,' he said grimly. 'How far out are you? Ten minutes? Get in as fast as you can without taking any stupid risks. Bring your wife straight down to the jetty. We'll be waiting for you. . . No, the hospital's not operating yet. The only facilities are on board the *Mandala*. . .'

He paused. The voice at the other end was clearly expostulating.

'No,' Ryan said flatly. 'If there's bleeding, then there's no time to get to Batarra. Come to the jetty. Now!'

He slammed down the phone.

'Who?' Rose said quietly, dreading the answer.

'Elizabeth Sullivan.'

Rose closed her eyes. 'I sent her to stay with her mother in Batarra two weeks ago.'

'You didn't check that she'd gone?'

Rose's eyes flew wide. 'No.'

'Well, you should have.'

'That's unfair,' Rose said quietly. 'She said she was going. I outlined the risks if she stayed. Do you expect me to go round to her house once a night and make sure she hasn't come home?'

'They've decided to have a home birth instead.' Ryan was moving towards the door as he spoke and Rose went with him. 'They didn't mention the plan to you?'

'They asked me if I'd help,' Rose admitted. 'But I thought it was madness. It's their first child and the nearest hospital's two hours away—plus, I'm not an obstetrician. I told both of them what they were risking and thought they agreed with me. Home births might be an option if you live with close medical help—but to have one here. . .'

'Well, it seems they tried it anyway,' Ryan said grimly. 'She's been in labour for twenty-four hours, getting nowhere, and now there's bleeding.'

'Oh, no.' Rose looked fearfully up at him.

'We might be in trouble. If we need to operate. . .'

Rose thought swiftly. To do an emergency Caesarean here. . .

Caesarean operations needed three doctors—or at the very least two doctors and a very skilled nurse. One as anaesthetist. One to operate, and one to receive and revive the baby if necessary.

'You know the nurses available,' Ryan snapped, guessing her thoughts. 'Can we contact any of them?'

'I can try,' Rose said doubtfully. 'But they'll probably all be up at Batarra.'

'Try.' Ryan picked the phone up from the floor of the future sister's station and handed it to her. 'Fast.'

There was no one. Each phone call rang out unanswered, and Rose and Ryan wasted no more time. Ryan ushered Rose into the passenger seat of his car and they reached the jetty just as an ancient utility truck pulled to a screeching halt. Wayne Sullivan had taken Ryan at his word. He had wasted no time.

His wife was on the seat beside him. Ryan reached the utility as it drew to a halt and swung the door wide to reveal a woman huddled and fearful.

They needed a stretcher. Rose was already flying towards the first-aid room. She came back at a run. The men seized her flimsy stretcher and carefully moved the woman on to it.

Once on board the *Mandala*, a swift examination confirmed their worst fears. Rose put her stethoscope to the woman's abdomen and looked up to Ryan, her eyes a question as he finished an internal examination.

'Meconium staining,' he said. 'And hardly any dilation. Heartbeat?'

'It's unsteady.' Rose's own heart wasn't feeling too steady either. This was the worst nightmare of a country GP. 'Faint. . .'

'We operate,' Ryan said decisively. He moved to the head of the table and took the frightened woman's hands. 'Elizabeth. . .'

A low moan was their only response.

'Elizabeth, your baby's in trouble,' Ryan said. His voice was gentle but firm. 'You're hardly dilated. There's no way it can be born naturally and live. The heartbeat's fading. We have to do a Caesarean.'

'No.' Elizabeth shook her head wildly.

'Get Wayne in,' Ryan told Rose. He turned back to Elizabeth. 'Elizabeth, it's your only chance for a healthy baby. There's no choice.'

'We have to do it, Liz.' It was the husband. He had

walked in as Rose opened the door, but had clearly heard from the adjoining room what was going on. 'Come on, love. You've tried hard enough.' He looked from Rose to Ryan. 'She wanted. . . She wanted it so bad to be just us.'

'I won't have a Caesarean,' the woman sobbed. 'Just let me be. I told you you shouldn't have brought me here, Wayne. I told you. . .'

'Elizabeth, listen,' Ryan ordered. He put his stethoscope in the woman's ears and lifted her so he could place the other end on her abdomen. 'Listen.'

The woman looked fearfully up and her husband moved swiftly to take her hands. 'Come on, love.'

She listened. Her face was drenched in sweat and her eyes were pain-filled but she listened.

'That's your baby's heartbeat,' Ryan said. 'And it's fading. You have to let us do something.'

'I don't want to be cut.' The woman fell back. 'Wayne, don't let them. Don't let them. . .'

'Mrs Sullivan, stop acting like a spoilt child.' Ryan's voice cut across her mounting hysteria. 'Do you want this baby or not?'

'I. . .' She looked wildly up to her husband, looking for support. Wisely he turned to face Ryan. 'I don't want. . .'

'I know what you don't want,' Ryan snapped. 'I'm asking you, do you want a live baby?'

There was a long silence. 'Yes,' she whispered finally.

'Then we have to do a Caesarean. Now.'

'But I'm frightened.'

'There's no need for you to be frightened. Dr O'Meara is a competent anaesthetist, and I've done this operation plenty of times.'

'You'll put me to sleep?'

'Yes.' Ryan grimaced as he spoke and Rose knew why. If they'd been able to perform a Caesarean under epidural anaesthetic then Elizabeth would remain awake—and Rose wouldn't be tied to monitoring her breathing. She could pay some attention to the baby when it was born. An epidural, though, required patient co-operation, and Elizabeth was not to be trusted to give them that. She was hysterical enough already.

'OK,' Ryan snapped. 'Let's go.'

'Will. . .will I wait outside?' Wayne Sullivan asked fearfully, and Ryan shook his head.

'We're going to need you,' he said. 'Scrub here and then I'm going to give you a fast lesson in reviving a newborn before we start.'

'I. . .we read some books.'

'Fine,' Ryan said grimly. 'I hope they were the right ones.'

It was as nasty a little episode as Rose had experienced. Elizabeth wept herself into the anaesthesia, blocking her passages in the process and making Rose's job doubly hard. Rose concentrated fiercely. Ryan moved swiftly but there was no baby's cry at the end.

The baby was born limp and blue. Ryan handed the tiny body over to his waiting father.

'Suck his airways clear like I showed you,' he snapped. 'And then breathe him.' He turned back to his patient. There was nothing else he could do. The wound under his hands was bleeding profusely and he couldn't pay anything else any attention.

Rose looked over to where Wayne fumbled with the tiny arrival, wishing desperately she could leave her air-hose and help. She couldn't. Without both Rose and Ryan, the woman on the table beneath their hands would die.

And when Ryan finally stopped the bleeding and turned to grasp the lifeless infant and massage and breathe for him, they all knew it was too late.

'Oh, God,' Wayne breathed, his face crumpling as he looked down at the body of his little son. 'Oh, dear

God. I don't know how. . . I don't know how I'm
going to tell her.'

They didn't have to. Elizabeth's breathing had
resumed. Her eyes flickered open and she looked
straight at her husband and then down to her baby.

'He's dead, isn't he?' she said flatly.

'Yes,' Ryan said gently. 'I'm sorry Mrs Sullivan. His
heart just gave out.'

She stared up at Ryan and then looked again at her
husband. Slowly she held out her arms. 'Give him to
me. . .'

Her husband moved forward and placed the baby on
the coverlet at her side. The woman stared down at his
tiny features and her face worked. She touched him
lightly, once, and then turned back to Ryan.

'You killed him,' she said flatly. 'I knew you would.
You doctors are all the same. You bastards. . .'

Rose was loading a syringe. She looked a question
at Ryan and he gave an almost imperceptible nod and
walked out of the room. Swiftly Rose drove the needle
home, before Elizabeth had a chance to argue. Ergo-
metrine and a sedative. . .'Mrs Sullivan, we did all we
could do,' Rose said gently. 'We're really very, very
sorry.'

'Leave me alone,' the woman whispered. 'Just leave
us. . .'

There was nothing else they could do. Rose nodded,
gave a brief sympathetic glance across at the white-
faced husband who had to deal with this, and left them.

Ryan was standing out on the deck. He was still
gowned and gloved. As Rose approached he pulled his
gloves off and flung them on to the deck. It was as
though he were discarding his medicine—discarding
what had happened in the little theatre.

'Ryan. . .' Rose put a hand on his arm. Her formerly
fleeting impression of solitude deepened. 'Ryan, there

was nothing else we could have done. We. . . It was just too late.'

'She'll blame us until the day she dies.'

'Yes.' Rose nodded. 'But the alternative is to blame herself and I think. . . Maybe she'd go crazy if she had to do that. So we wear it.'

He turned to her, then. 'You sound like a doctor of twenty years' standing.'

'That's how I feel tonight,' Rose confessed. 'Old and tired.'

'Hell!' He turned away, seizing the handrail and staring bleakly out over the estuary. 'This is why I came here,' he confessed. 'City practice. . . I saw one wealthy, elderly patient after another, and I thought here. . .here I could do some good. Make amends. . .'

'Amends?' Rose frowned but he wasn't listening.

'So here I am, ready to be needed, and what happens? I spend my day listening to people belly-aching about imaginary ills while the one person who needs me is damned if she'll come close. And a child dies.'

'It had to be their choice.'

'Stupid. . .' He closed his eyes as if in pain. 'I can't get away from it. People still do crazy, criminally stupid things. Throwing away life. . .'

'They always will,' Rose said gently. 'We can't stop them.'

'We can do something, though,' Ryan snapped. 'A competent sister breathing that baby might have saved its life.'

'I don't know,' Rose said doubtfully. 'Ryan, you can't tell.'

'I know if they'd been able to come straight to a hospital with trained staff then the baby would have stood a better chance. So. . .'

'So?'

'So we leave for Brisbane on Monday. We get this place registered.'

'But. . .' Rose stared at him. 'Ryan. . . Dr Connell, have you thought? We can't leave Kora Bay without anyone.'

'I'll get a locum here.'

'You can do that?'

'With money, anything's possible,' Ryan said grimly. 'But I want that hospital ready by Monday, Dr O'Meara.'

She stared. Six days. . .

And then she thought of the limp, lifeless baby she would soon have to deal with and she knew that Ryan was right. The facilities were ready. Not to have them operating for lack of physical effort was criminal.

'It'll be ready,' she told him.

Ryan drove Rose home without speaking. It was as if the pain of the night had turned from the childless couple to the doctor who had tried so hard to save their baby. He was a man in pain, and Rose saw and wondered.

She couldn't help. He wouldn't let her near. She bade him goodnight and he gave her a bleak nod, turned the car and left her alone.

It was a long time before Rose slept that night. Despite physical exhaustion, her overworked mind wouldn't stop. Finally she gave up the attempt. As the night reached its darkest, Rose walked down across the headland and on to the ocean beach.

This had been Rose's beach as a child. This beach had been her playground, her treasure-trove and her sanctuary. She sat on the sand and listened to the whisper of the waves, and the events of the night moved back into perspective. A wrong decision. A dead child. There was nothing more she could have done, though, and she knew that. She only wished she could believe Ryan felt the same.

Where was he now? Pacing the deck of the *Mandala*? An ambulance had collected Elizabeth Sullivan and taken her to the Batarra hospital. She had left still berating Ryan Connell, and Rose knew it had hurt.

She wished. Oh, she wished she could be with him. That she could take the haunted look from his eyes as she had done once before.

Her place was not by his side, though. Ryan Connell wanted no woman. He wanted no one.

Finally, weary beyond belief, Rose stood and walked slowly up the sandy track to her cottage. She stood on the back veranda and watched the star-lit black sky over the ocean. Brisbane on Monday. . . The city. And then? Then Kora Bay and her beloved cottage and her beach forever.

The thought gave her no comfort at all. Kora Bay no longer seemed her home. Her home was Ryan Connell.

CHAPTER EIGHT

Roy collected Rose just before dawn on Monday morning. In the stillness before dawn Rose heard the car come up from the marina, and was standing, suitcase ready, out on the road.

Roy greeted her warmly. 'It's a great morning,' he told her as he restarted the car. 'We'll have a good run down to Brisbane.'

'Mmm.' Rose swallowed, wondering again just what this unassuming man thought of her. She glanced across at him and fingered her shorts. As they'd be spending the day at sea she had thought they were appropriate, but now. . .'Maybe I. . . I should have worn something a bit more. . .'

'You look great to me,' Roy said seriously. He glanced over at Rose and saw the disquiet on her face. 'Beats what they call "designer casuals". We had a woman come on board wearing a white marine jacket— and she got grease on it. You'd think the end of the world had come.'

'If I got grease on these I wouldn't even notice,' Rose smiled, her tension easing. Then, unable to stop herself, she asked, 'Does. . . Did Ryan entertain much on board?'

'He used to,' Roy told her. 'Before the fire. Least. . .' He stopped, considering. 'Maybe it wasn't Ryan,' he said. 'Ryan's wife was a great one for entertaining. I sometimes thought Ryan didn't want any part of it. It was all for Sarah's sake.'

'Ryan's wife. . .' Rose's voice was a whisper. 'I. . . I didn't know Ryan was married.'

Roy shook his head and looked across at Rose, his eyes sympathetic. 'He's not,' he told her firmly. 'Not

134

any more. Divorce came through six months ago. And
good riddance, I'd say. Damnedest piece of work he's
ever got mixed up with.'

'You didn't like her?' Rose knew she shouldn't be
asking these questions, but in the intimacy of the near
dark and the warmth of the car interior it seemed
strangely OK. And Roy seemed eager to talk.

'Did at first,' Roy said bluntly. 'Well, everyone did.
Sarah'd charm the poison out of a snake if she set her
mind to it. Only, after they were married she didn't see
any need to charm me, so I guess I saw a side of her
Ryan wasn't shown. Until the fire. . .'

'The fire?'

The car was drawing up at the marina and Roy shook
his head. 'I spend my life speaking out of turn,' he said
firmly. He grinned. 'Some time I guess I'll even tell
you about the fire—but not now.' He motioned to
where Ryan was standing, a lone figure aboard the
Mandala, silhouetted against the dawn sky. 'Since the
night you delivered the dead baby he's been like a bear
with a sore head and I'm not the man to keep a sore-
headed bear waiting.'

It was a fast trip south. Ryan was wasting no time. He
stood at the wheel and concentrated as though he could
will Brisbane to be closer.

'We could have flown,' Rose offered. 'It would have
been faster.'

Ryan shook his head. 'We'll be down there by
tomorrow morning. We can do what we have to
without the need for hotels, and then return fast.'

It was seldom Ryan saw a need to speak to Rose,
and Rose just as surely saw no need to exchange
pleasantries with Ryan. If Ryan was at the wheel, Rose
put her nose into her big text on family medicine and
studied.

'They might ask a few practical questions,' Ryan had
warned her. 'Brush up.'

Rose wasn't sure if his warning was just to keep her occupied—out of his hair.

She offered to take her turn at the wheel and, rather to her surprise, her offer was accepted. It was a good feeling to have trust, she decided. For Rose, brought up in the chauvinistic society of Kora Bay, the feeling was a novelty. These men treated her as an equal.

Roy treated her as more than that. He treated her as a friend.

'Coffee?' It was Roy's turn at the wheel but he'd set the automatic pilot and gone below, emerging three minutes later with two mugs of coffee. He carried one to where Rose was curled on a deck chair studying. 'Uugh. . .' Rose was memorising the latest treatment of diabetic complications. The accompanying photographs were gruesome and Roy grimaced. 'I thought there was some rule about light reading on deck.' He tried another look. 'Good grief. Is that really what happens if you have diabetes?'

'Only if you neglect yourself.' Rose smiled. Then she took pity on him. 'Even then not very often.'

'What a warning!'

'The first obstetric textbook I read put me off childbirth for life.' Rose smiled. 'It spent twenty pages on normal pregnancies and the following seven hundred on abnormalities. By the time I finished, I figured every second baby I delivered would have two heads or none at all.' She took her coffee. 'Thank you,' she said, and then smiled shyly. 'And thank you for being nice to me.'

Roy smiled and went back to the wheel. 'There's no need to thank me,' he told her. 'It's a pleasure to have someone to talk to. It can get bloody lonely sometimes. Even lonelier than when I worked the fences at Bindenalong.'

'Bindenalong?'

Roy frowned. He looked towards the cabin but Ryan was behind closed doors. 'The Doc's farm.'

'Did Ryan inherit it?' Rose frowned.

'Yeah. Well, he came into it unexpectedly. It was his uncle's farm, and his uncle and cousin were killed in a car crash. Doc came down from Brisbane and took over. The farm was a bit of a mess, but Doc Connell pulled the place together something terrific—especially as he still worked during the week in Brisbane. He found a great manager. . .' And then Roy caught himself, as though suddenly remembering something distasteful. He looked down at his charts and then crossed to Rose. 'Do you reckon we ought to head out along here? The map says it's getting pretty shallow.'

It was a ruse to change the subject, but Rose accepted it. 'We should be right if we stick close to the shelf. If we cut out it's going to be a darn sight rougher and it'll take longer.'

'Yeah, OK.' Roy relaxed. 'I ought to be better than this by now,' he told her. 'But the sea still makes me nervous.'

'You're not accustomed to it?'

'Nope.' Roy grinned. 'I was a boundary rider at Bindenalong. We had some trouble with poddy rustlers, and one of them shot a ruddy great hole in my leg. The leg's useless for rough work now, so I took myself off to the city and did a bookkeeping course.'

'The leg's been rebuilt?'

'Yeah. . .' He grimaced. 'Tib and fib both shattered, and the knee-cap wasn't recognisable as such. They pulled it out in splinters. I was darned lucky not to lose the leg. My knee-cap's now a nice metal plate. Sends the metal detectors berserk in airports.'

Rose's eyes widened. 'You must have had good surgeons not to lose the leg.'

'Yeah, well, thanks to Ryan,' Roy said grimly. 'He paid for everything, and then, after I finished the bookkeeping course, he found me and offered me this job.'

'Ryan found you. . .?'

'Yeah.' Roy shifted uncomfortably. 'I didn't hear from him for months. Makes him sound like he didn't care in the first place, doesn't it? It's not true. The poddy-rustling happened just before the fire. Ryan had so much on his plate then—well, he made sure I was financially OK and as soon as he could he came to find me.'

'Roy!'

Unnoticed, Ryan had appeared at the cabin door behind them.

'Could I see you for a moment, please?' Ryan's tone was grim, but Roy grinned at Rose and winked. 'Can you take over, Captain?' He smiled and left her to it.

Rose didn't mind. The *Mandala* was magnificent. The day was perfect, hot and clear, with the sunlight glittering on the turquoise sea. She felt like moving her hand down hard on the throttle and heading out fast, away, away to Africa or Hawaii. She didn't want to go to Brisbane. She didn't want what was before her. Soon this moment would cease and she would have to stand before the Medical Board and plead for a future that, without Ryan Connell, she hardly wanted. . .

She shook herself in anger. What on earth was she thinking? How could she not want Kora Bay—not want her medicine?

'I do want them,' she whispered. 'I just want Ryan Connell more. . .'

They docked at Brisbane early the next morning and before they had even moored Rose was feeling uncomfortable. Brisbane was *Mandala's* home port, and people here knew Ryan Connell. He was hailed and greeted by name by at least half a dozen yacht-owners as *Mandala* was manouevred into her berth.

'Hey, Ryan!' A man about Ryan's age, smoothly good-looking and immaculately groomed, leapt from the deck of a nearby yacht and strolled along the jetty to greet them. 'Welcome back. Hi, Roy.' He eyed

Rose critically as she tied the stern rope to the bollard. 'I told you you'd need more crew.'

'Ed, this is Rose O'Meara,' Ryan told him. 'Rose, Dr Ed Matherson. Rose isn't crew. She's a friend.'

Ed raised his eyes. 'You could have fooled me,' he said softly, his eyes running over Rose's slim form in a manner Rose found offensive. 'Bit of a change, eh, Ryan?' Then, as Ryan's brow snapped down in anger, Ed smiled placatingly. 'OK, Ryan. I know. You're just good friends, and I'll bet Roy here makes a great chaperon. He's always been the soul of discretion.' He eyed Rose again and spoke almost absentmindedly. 'You'll be coming up to the hospital to see Vincent, I guess. I'll tell him to expect you. He's been in after scar excision. Oh, and Sarah's in town.'

'Sarah!' Ryan's eyes, which had been angry before, were now cold as well. He turned away. 'Thanks for the information, Ed. If you'll excuse us.' He walked back into the cabin and slammed the door.

'Temper's no better,' Ed said amiably. He grinned across at Roy. 'I don't know how you put up with him.' He sat down on the edge of the jetty as if intent on a good gossip and eyed Rose again. 'Tell me about you,' he said to Rose. 'Where did our Ryan pick you up?'

'Rose!' It was a curt order from inside the cabin and Rose welcomed it. She didn't like this man and she didn't like the way his eyes appraised her. Thankfully she followed Ryan inside.

Ryan was behind the bar, pouring himself a drink, and his scarred hand was clenching his glass so tightly that Rose half expected it to shatter. 'Get yourself ready,' he snapped. 'We're going shopping.'

Rose stood stock-still. 'What do you mean?'

'I said we're going shopping,' Ryan repeated. 'We'll get you out of those damned shorts.'

'I have a skirt.' Rose tried for dignity but it didn't quite come off. 'And if you're so ashamed of me, then I don't see. . .'

'I'm not the least ashamed.' Ryan slammed the glass down on the bar and his drink splashed over the side. 'But that. . . Ed Matherson. . .is an example of what you're going to have to face. The Medical Board is old-school, so you have to be conservative and acceptable. You've stepped out of the role you're supposed to play—so now it's up to you to show you're penitent, capable and confident. So. . . So we get you looking confident.'

'Shoulder-pads,' Rose grimaced, and Ryan managed a smile.

'I think we can do without power-dressing. But to succeed you'll need to be successful on their terms. Believe me, Rose, it's a façade but one you have to apply. The people doing the work for us on hospital accreditation have organised a cocktail party tonight. We need to appear together—a team of competent professionals. So I'm taking you shopping.'

'You. . .? No way!'

Ryan shook his head. 'We do this my way,' he said coldly. 'I brought you down to Brisbane to get you registered and to get the hospital registered. You brought your funeral suit, I suppose?'

'So what? It's a perfectly good suit.'

'It might have been ten years ago. It's not now.'

'It'll do,' Rose snapped. 'I'm not going to buy some fancy outfit I'll never wear again. I don't. . .'

'I'm paying.'

'You're not paying for my clothes!'

'Try stopping me.'

Rose drew in her breath. 'I'm not your kept woman, Ryan Connell, regardless of what Ed Matherson thinks. I'm damned if I'm accepting charity from you.'

'You're not accepting charity. You're in my employ and you need uniforms for this damned interview and cocktail do.'

Rose took a deep breath. 'Look, this has gone far

enough. Thank you for the ride, but I'll leave you now. I'm not taking any more from you. . .'

Ryan was looking at her, his cold eyes watchful. There was a hint of perplexity at the back of his eyes. 'For heaven's sake, Rose. I have enough money not to notice one or two dresses.'

'You might not notice, but I would,' Rose flung at him. 'I'm not beholden to any man. I'm free, Ryan Connell, and that's the way I mean it to stay.'

'I know you are.' Ryan's tone suddenly gentled. 'Do you think I don't know that? My wild and free woman. . .'

'I am not your woman!' Rose was yelling now, impervious to any sound that might carry up to Roy and the obnoxious Ed. 'I am not your woman, Ryan Connell! I want nothing to do with you. I accepted your help, but not at the expense of. . .'

'Of your pride?' Ryan's voice was still gentle. He walked over and took her hands in his. 'Rose, don't do this. I know you hate charity. Well, believe it or not, this is not charity I'm offering. I need you to work with me. I can't keep practising alone and I want you to be my partner. Now. . . If you insist on paying me back for what I outlay on your appearance, that's fine, but now. . . For now, you do what I tell you. I know what these men—they're all men you'll be facing, Rose—I know how they react. It's wrong, but it's the way it is. If you were a man I'd say go out and get yourself an expensive suit. Clothes matter.'

'But it stinks.'

'The system stinks,' Ryan agreed. 'But let's get you into the system before you try changing it.'

It seemed that Rose had never shopped in her life. To shop. . . Until now, shopping had meant a visit to the supermarket. Shopping with Ryan Connell took on a whole new dimension.

They caught a cab through the city to a wide back-

street in an obviously wealthy outer suburb. Rose
stared with astonishment at the place where they pulled
up. Set in a tree-lined residential street, the elegant
terrace looked like an expensive home. The sign at the
front said simply, 'Caroline's'. Ryan took Rose's hand
in his, ignoring her reluctance, and led her up the
paved garden path.

Rose looked down at her shorts with horror. She had
wanted to change into her skirt but Ryan had said
simply, 'You wear that skirt over my dead body. The
shorts we can get away with, but the skirt's
inexcusable.'

'I can't go in here,' Rose whispered frantically to
Ryan as he placed his hand on the bell. 'I look. . .'

'You look great,' Ryan told her. 'Put your nose in
the air, Rose O'Meara, pretend you're the queen of
the world and you're made. Apologise once to these
people and you're doomed. If you're dressed differ-
ently, then it's the rest of the world that's made the
mistake—not you!'

The door swung open and an immaculately groomed
woman of about Ryan's age stood before them. When
she saw Ryan her face broke into wreaths of smiles.

'Ryan. Darling, how are you? I haven't seen you
since Sarah. . .' She broke off, aware suddenly that
Ryan was holding another woman by the hand. Swiftly,
and as if consigning memories to where they belonged,
she seized Ryan's free hand in hers. 'It's lovely to see
you,' she said, and by her voice Rose knew that she
was sincere. 'I thought maybe you mightn't. . . But. . .
Well, come in.' For the first time she really looked at
Rose and her smile encompassed the girl at Ryan's
side. 'How may I help you?'

Rose had to admire her. It was as if the woman
hadn't even noticed Rose's tatty shorts. In this elegant
salon Rose's battered clothes looked ridiculous, but
the woman didn't show by as much as a glance that she
was aware of it.

'We thought you might be the lady to help us, Caroline,' Ryan smiled. He held Rose's hand firmly in his and smiled down at her disreputable outfit. 'Caroline Vincent—Rose O'Meara. Rose is a medico from Kora Bay, where I'm now settled.' His smile deepened. The look in his eyes was caressing and proprietary, leaving the owner of this elegant boutique in no doubt as to the relationship of the two before her. 'Rose made a last-moment decision to join me and now refuses to leave the confines of the *Mandala* because she's not dressed for the city. So we came to you.'

The woman's eyes widened. Her gaze went once more to Rose, assessing her slim figure, her wide green eyes and her startling mass of hair. 'Well, it would be a real pleasure to dress you,' she said softly. 'More than one outfit, my dear?'

Rose went to speak, but Ryan was before her. 'Of course more than one outfit,' he said definitely. And then, as Rose's mouth moved, Ryan placed a finger on her lips in a gesture of affectionately silencing her. 'We have a business meeting this afternoon and a party this evening. And no nonsense about you paying, my lovely Rose. I refused to let you bring the clothes you so desperately wanted to pack, so I'm picking up the tab.' He smiled across at Caroline. 'Make them something special, Caroline. I want the lady to do me proud.'

The owner of the shop smiled from Ryan to Rose. 'If I may say so, Ryan,' she said gently, 'I think she already does. Now, Rose, where shall we start?'

'Ryan. . .'

'Rose, just shut up and do as you're told,' Ryan said fondly, but his eyes were giving Rose another, firmer message.

'Oh, and I was expecting such a dull, dull morning,' Caroline said happily, unaware of the undercurrents of the situation. 'Ryan, there's coffee and the morning

papers on the stand behind you. Make yourself
comfortable. Rose and I are going to have fun.'

Rose had never seen clothes like these. The tourist
shops of Kora Bay had expensive clothes, but these
were a class above even those highly priced items. The
clothes Caroline produced screamed quality at first
glance.

'They're all one-off designer labels,' Caroline told
her, producing a simple silk dress in a stunning aqua-
marine for her to inspect. 'With your colouring this
would look fabulous.' She smiled at Rose. 'Let's try.'

Rose fingered the label and found no price. She
looked a query. 'Is it very expensive?' she asked
tentatively. 'I don't. . . I don't want Ryan spending too
much.'

Caroline laughed and shook her head. 'My dear, you
don't need to worry about price when Ryan Connell is
paying,' she said simply. 'Ryan pays for quality, and as
long as he gets it, that's all that matters. He'd have my
hide if I showed you anything less than the best.' She
smiled happily. 'What I'd give to have a man like Ryan
Connell look at me the way he looks at you. . .'

Rose fell silent. She felt trapped in a silken web, and
the web was tightening. . .

The dress turned Rose into someone she didn't
know. Caroline produced soft silk underclothes, and
the dress slid over them like a caress. Rose turned to
the mirror in astonishment.

The silk clung softly to her slim form, accentuating
the curves of her body and making her every inch a
woman. For years Rose had blocked out the fact that
she was a woman with a woman's needs, but this dress
would not let her forget it. The neckline fell deep to
reveal the outward curve of her breasts. Tiny sleeves
made her arms seem softer and slimmer than they'd
ever seemed before. The dress clung until just below
the waist and then flared out to fall almost to ankle

length in masses of soft folds. The shimmering green-blue of the dress lit up Rose's eyes and added depth and lustre to her mass of hair.

'My dear,' Caroline said breathlessly. 'This is right. . .'

And so were the elegant Italian sandals to go with it.

'Perfect,' Caroline pronounced. 'Do you want to show Ryan?'

'He'll see soon enough,' Rose said bitterly.

Caroline smiled. 'OK, then. Now the meeting.'

She produced a linen suit and a soft apricot silk shirt. 'And a scarf to tie back those curls for business,' Caroline said, wrinkling her nose in distaste at anything so dull. 'But I think you're right to let your hair free at other times.' She touched Rose's chestnut mane enviously. 'With a natural beauty like this. . .' She fingered the ends. 'Maybe, though. . . Chelsea next door is a hairdresser. Would you like me to ask her to pop over? The ends have dried a little with your exposure to the sea. She could just trim. . .'

'You don't touch the hair.' It was Ryan, coming through from the hall to stand and watch the two women. His eyes went over Rose with careful scrutiny. She was dressed in the suit and she looked. . . She looked like someone from a magazine, Rose thought grimly. She didn't look like Rose O'Meara. Ryan nodded slowly. 'I thought. . .' he started, and then stopped as if catching himself. 'Is this all you've decided on?' he asked roughly.

Caroline smiled and shook her head. 'We have the most beautiful cocktail dress,' she assured him. 'Just exquisite. I couldn't persuade Rose to come out and show you. We only have to choose shoes to match this. . .'

'Fine.' The warmth had faded from Ryan's eyes and he looked at his watch.

Rose was aware of a sharp stab of disappointment. She turned back to the mirror. Somehow. . . Somehow in these clothes she had felt, just for a moment, that she might have a chance. Cinderella had changed into a beautiful dress and Prince Charming had fallen in love with her. Ryan's brusqueness showed clearly that such a thing wasn't for Rose.

'I'll be fast,' she promised dully. She started to take the jacket off.

'Leave it on,' Caroline urged. 'If you're going to the meeting this afternoon you might as well, and it looks smashing.' She turned to Ryan, and her face tightened suddenly, as if she found what she wanted to say difficult. 'Are you. . .will you see Allan while you're in town?'

'I might,' Ryan said non-committally.

'He'd be pleased to see you.' Caroline hesitated. 'He's changed so much. I know it's hard, Ryan, but he doesn't get many visitors. They operated last week to excise scar tissue at the back of his knees. Now they think he'll be able to walk. . .'

Vincent. . . Allan Vincent. Rose looked from Caroline to Ryan, but no explanation ensued. Then Caroline had turned back to her, her wide smile encompassing her.

'Smashing,' she repeated in satisfaction. 'But I haven't heard you tell her that yet, Ryan Connell. If you don't know enough by now to tell a woman she looks wonderful when she does, then I wash my hands of you. Now, does Rose look wonderful, or does she not?'

Ryan looked over at Rose, his eyes still strangely distant. 'She does,' he said slowly. 'But then, she always has.'

CHAPTER NINE

'WHO is Allan Vincent?' Rose asked as they were once more in the taxi. It seemed easier than talking of clothes. . .or her forthcoming meeting with the Brisbane medical establishment.

'The ex-manager of my property,' Ryan said shortly. 'Caroline's brother.'

'And he's ill?'

'He was burned in the same fire I was injured in. His burns were a darned sight worse than mine, and his legs were crushed by a falling beam. Can you cope with a visit to a rehabilitation hospital?'

'Of course.'

They found Allan Vincent concentrating fiercely on his feet. He was in a bright, superbly equipped gymnasium set on the ground floor of an obviously exclusive private hospital. As Rose and Ryan entered he was alone in the gym, gripping two long parallel bars as if his life depended on it, and cursing in even rhythm to the piped music coming through the speakers in the physio-therapy centre.

His face, when he raised it to see who approached, was scarred more severely than Ryan's, the edges of each skin-graft still clearly delineated. Burn scars often resembled patchwork at this stage of healing, Rose knew, until the worst of the scarring could be smoothed by further surgery. The modern method of constricting bandages during healing meant that the final result would be presentable, but even so, it would be a long and painful business. . .

There was still plenty of surgery ahead of Allan Vincent. Burns. . . They were damnable injuries.

147

Uninjured skin was used for skin-grafts. Skin-grafts were applied and then plastic surgery was needed to fix the scarring—back and back to Theatre, until patients were sick to death of hospitals. By the look of Allan's scars he was lucky to be alive.

'Allan,' Ryan said coolly, and Rose's eyes flicked up to his. Not a lot of affection, then. . .

'Ryan!' Allan Vincent's scarred face twisted. Rose had thought he was older, but his eyes were young and vulnerable.

A white-coated girl whose badge said, 'Lyn Spender, Physiotherapist', materialised from the office at the side of the gym. She pushed a wheelchair. 'If you have visitors then we'll let you off doing more, Mr Vincent.' She smiled at Allan and her smile was warm. 'Double this afternoon.'

'Slave-driver,' Allan muttered, but his voice held affection. Obviously he and this pert young physio-therapist knew each other well. 'I'm damned if I'm trying again today. I've had enough.'

'It takes patience.'

'It takes a lifetime, more like.' Allan slumped into the wheelchair the girl had placed into position, and the physiotherapist moved discreetly away. He gestured to Rose. 'Who's this? Successor for Sarah?'

'Would you blame me if it was?' Ryan's voice was suddenly intense and Rose grimaced. What was he saying?

Allan's eyes travelled over Rose. Using his hands, he lifted his legs on to the foot plate, wincing with the effort. 'No,' he said slowly. 'I wouldn't blame you. You know that, Ryan.'

'I know that.' Ryan's tone suddenly softened. 'This is yet another doctor, though, Allan. Dr Rose O'Meara.'

'Yeah?' Allan's eyes lightened. 'A doctor? Makes a change from the lot here. If I spend much more time with Dr Ed Matherson, I'm likely to brain him.'

'There have to be brains present in the first place to do that.' Ryan grinned, and Allan gave a crack of laughter. Then he winced again. 'Bad?' Ryan asked.

'Yeah.' He sighed. 'It'd almost be easier spending the rest of my life in a wheelchair. By the time the fractures were stable the skin-grafts had almost healed, but the scars set in hard, unyielding ridges. If anyone had told me that when my legs healed I'd have to be operated on to remove the scars. . .'

'Life's a learning process,' Ryan said lightly, and his hand came down on the younger man's shoulder for a fraction of a moment. It was enough to make Allan's face change colour.

'The staff here aren't all bad,' Ryan continued. He gestured over to where Lyn's head was bent over her desk. 'Your torturer-in-chief seems OK.'

'My. . .' Allan's eyes turned to where Ryan looked and he gave a rueful smile. 'Oh, Lyn. Yeah. She's. . . well, she's OK.'

'Just OK?' It was teasing, but Allan didn't see that. The flush became angry, and Rose could see that Ryan was pressing on a nerve.

'Yeah. OK. Leave it, Ryan.'

Ryan nodded, his eyes carefully appraising. He knew the younger man was hurting, and not just physically. 'What are your plans when you leave hospital?' he asked mildly.

'I haven't thought. . .'

'That's nonsense. Of course you've thought.'

Allan stared down at his feet. 'Of course I've thought,' he muttered. 'Yeah. . .'

'And?'

'And what I do depends on my big sister,' Allan said savagely. 'Caroline's house, Caroline's money, Caroline's life. . . No one's going to employ me looking like this.'

'I will.'

'You. . .?'

'The current manager of Bindenalong is hopeless. The men don't like him and they liked you. You know the work's mainly administration. We can get a three-wheel farm bike instead of a horse, and I can't see many problems. How about coming back at the end of the year?'

Allan stared. 'But. . .'

'But what?'

'But you're. . .' He looked at Rose. 'Sarah. . .'

'I wish to hell Sarah could be forgotten,' Ryan said grimly. 'She can't, but I'm damned if I can see why she should go on wrecking lives. I'm serious about the offer.'

Allan's face slowly changed. 'You'd do that. . .?'

'I'd do that.'

Allan's eyes turned back to where Lyn's fair curls bobbed over the window of the office. What he was thinking was as transparent as the glass. Ryan grinned.

'Think about it,' he said, laying his hand on Allan's shoulder, and then he looked up and grimaced as Ed Matherson strode through the door towards them. 'And here's our favourite doctor,' he said softly.

Allan looked up and saw Ed, and his face closed.

'They told me at the office you were here.' Ed beamed at Ryan. His gaze swung to Rose and his eyes widened. 'Well, well. . .' He whistled soundlessly. 'I begin to see. . .'

'You don't see anything at all,' Ryan snapped. 'We were just leaving.'

'Done our mercy visit for the month then, have we?' Ed smiled. He looked down at Allan. 'I'm sure you appreciate it, don't you, Allan?'

'Yes, thank you, Dr Matherson,' Allan said through gritted teeth, and Ed didn't even notice the sarcasm behind the mock-child's response.

'Take Mr Vincent back to the ward, will you, Miss Spender?' Ed called to the physiotherapist. 'Now, Ryan, how about coming back to my office for a drink?

Stay to lunch if you like.' Once more his eyes travelled over Rose. 'I'd enjoy that.'

'Sorry, but I came to see Allan.' Ryan shrugged Ed aside and turned back to grip Allan's hand. 'I'll be back,' he promised. 'Look after Miss Spender.'

'Blasted patronising moron. . .' Ryan had hardly got inside the taxi when he exploded in rage. 'If he can't see the harm he's doing. . .'

Rose knew exactly what he meant. To treat a man in a wheelchair like a child simply because he was in a wheelchair. . .

'And he's second-in-charge. . .' Ryan almost visibly ground his teeth. 'At least Allan's time in there is nearly over.'

'He was pleased with your job offer.'

Ryan gazed blankly at her and his face closed.

'I didn't know I was going to make it until I got there,' he said tightly. 'And I don't think I want to talk about it.'

They ate lunch in the city, at a quiet, comfortable restaurant where the waiters knew Ryan by name. Rose's feeling of disquiet was deepening by the minute. The thought of the inquisition ahead—her assessment by the Medical Board—was like a black cloud, and her clothes. . . Cinderella caught the wrong pumpkin, she thought bleakly.

'Why aren't you eating?' Ryan asked as Rose toyed with her salad.

'I'm not very hungry.'

'It won't be all that bad.'

'No?' Rose took a deep breath. 'Maybe not. But maybe this is normal for you. . . Meetings. . . Being dressed up like this. . .' She looked over to where he sat in his cool grey suit, every inch the successful professional. She knew in this outfit, in her lovely suit and with her hair tied back with a silk scarf, she fitted his image and looked the part she was to play. 'But this is not me, Ryan Connell. I've never spoken in public in my life before.'

'When you're angry you speak brilliantly,' Ryan said softly. 'So be angry.'

'I am angry.' Rose took a deep breath. 'I should be grateful to you but instead I feel as if I'm being dressed up like a Barbie doll.'

'If it's any consolation you don't look like a Barbie doll,' he told her, his mouth wryly smiling but his eye still distant. Then, as if he couldn't help himself, he brought his hand up to touch the soft swell of her breasts. His fingers came away as if burnt. 'Not a Barbie doll,' he said curtly.

Somehow Rose struggled through the interminable meeting. The feeling of being costumed and disguised as somebody else stayed with her, and the feeling actually helped. It was as if she were hiding behind a screen and could observe without being seen herself.

The meeting was structured very much as an exam, and that helped. The interview took place at the city's big teaching hospital. A few doctors were wearing sober business suits, but most appeared from the wards, white coats flapping and stethoscopes dangling from pockets. It made it clinical and familiar. Reassuring. . .

They knew Ryan and obviously he was respected, although Rose could see they were clearly puzzled as to why he should bury himself in a place like Kora Bay. Ryan stood and presented Rose's case in a clear, detached manner. Afterwards Rose was questioned. She answered as honestly as she could and the men were clearly impressed. They asked Rose to step outside while they made a decision and then she was recalled.

'Well, Dr O'Meara,' the chairman told her. 'This is irregular, but your action has been understandable—in fact in some ways commendable. If more of our young ones took their responsibilities to their parents and grandparents seriously it would make our jobs as medicos much easier. I think, given the evidence of your work in Kora Bay, we can pass registration.'

The other men nodded sagely in agreement and Rose, with a stroke of the chairman's pen, was qualified to practise medicine. She sat back with a gasp. Surely it shouldn't be this easy?

It seemed it was. Ryan collected her registration papers, bade the members of the board farewell, and ushered her out.

'There you are, Dr O'Meara,' he smiled. 'Nothing to it.'

'I don't believe it.'

'It's true.' He handed her the papers. 'Don't lose them.'

'I promise.' Rose clutched them to her and hesitated. They had emerged at the emergency entrance to the hospital. An ambulance screamed towards them, cut its siren as it entered the hospital precinct and drew to a halt twenty feet away. White coats swarmed out to meet it and Rose's feeling of unreality deepened. That was what she should be doing, rather than standing in these clothes with the afternoon before her.

Ryan's hand was already in the air as he hailed a cab. 'Ryan. . .'

'Yes?' A cab-driver had spotted them and was doing a perilous U-turn in the crowded traffic outside the hospital entrance.

'Ryan, I'm really grateful. . .'

'Well, repay the favour by giving a good impression tonight,' he said brusquely. 'I have formalities to deal with now, regarding the hospital registration. I'll be back at the *Mandala* at six-thirty to collect you for the cocktail party.'

'But. . .' Rose was interrupted. The cab had halted and a door was flung open.

'Get the cab to take you to the boat,' Ryan told her. 'The meeting I'm going to is on the other side of the city.' He propelled her firmly into the cab and closed the door.

Roy was waiting back at the boat. He opened the door to Rose and whistled silently. 'Wow!'

Rose flushed. 'Thank you,' she said stiffly.

'How did it go?'

'I'm registered.'

'So?' He frowned at her. 'You should be dancing on tables. Why no smile?'

'I guess. . .' Rose stooped to take her new shoes off and stood looking down at the beautiful leather. 'I guess I'm happy.'

'But you're not sure?'

Rose shook her head. 'I'm not,' she said honestly. She looked up at Roy's sympathetic eyes and the need to talk became almost overwhelming. 'Ryan. . . Ryan made me buy this. I feel so strange. And all those people. . . I'd forgotten what it was like. I couldn't cope, Roy.'

'You must have coped if you got yourself registered,' Roy reassured her. 'But I wouldn't have thought it'd worry you. You're not the sort of girl to be intimidated.'

'I know,' Rose whispered. 'But I don't fit here. . .'

'What the hell does that matter?' Roy demanded. 'You don't have to fit.' He eyed her speculatively. 'Unless. . .unless you think it's important to someone else that you fit. . .'

'I. . . I don't know what you mean,' Rose said breathlessly. 'Roy. . .'

'Now, I'm not a man to shove my nose in where it's not wanted,' Roy said softly. 'But am I right in thinking you're head over heels in love with one Ryan Connell?'

'Roy, I'm not. . . I can't be. . .' Rose broke off and

went to sink on to the big settee and put her face in her hands. 'This is so crazy. . .'

'Falling in love doesn't always make sense,' Roy told her. 'Happens just the same, though. I'm right, aren't I?'

'No. . . Yes!' Rose looked blindly up at the man above her. 'But Ryan doesn't want anything to do with me apart from professionally. He. . . He's being kind, but it's as if it's some sort of pay-out. Maybe he senses what I'm feeling for him and is reacting with pity. He keeps doing things for me, but there's. . .there's no caring. . .' Rose broke on a sob. 'What am I saying?' she whispered. 'What I'm saying is that he's doing things for me without love, and of course he is. He couldn't love me.'

'Why not?'

Rose looked wildly up at the concerned man before her. 'Because I'm not his class,' she said savagely. 'You know what I am? Rose O'Meara, of O'Meara Croc Cruises.' She fingered the silk of her blouse. 'The only decent clothes I possess are what he's bought me out of charity. He doesn't feel anything for me except pity.'

'Seems to me Ryan Connell doesn't know what the heck he's feeling,' Roy said firmly. 'I've known Ryan for a long time now, and this is the first time I've seen him act like this. Even with Sarah. . .'

Sarah. . . The shadow from the past. Ryan's wife. . .

'Tell me about Sarah, Roy,' Rose whispered, as though compelled. 'Did Ryan love her?'

'He thought he did,' Roy told her. The middle-aged secretary turned and walked behind the bar to pour two long, cool drinks. 'I ought to be doing book-work and keeping my mouth shut,' he said drily. He eyed Rose speculatively. 'But I'm not. Seems to me that you're the best thing that's come Ryan Connell's way in a long time, and I'm not a man to let a bit of misplaced sense of duty stand in the way of letting you know what you're up against.' He brought a drink round to Rose, perched on a bar stool and stared into his own drink. For a long moment Rose thought he wasn't going to start.

'Ryan was brought up hard,' Roy said eventually. 'His parents died when he was a kid, and his uncle didn't want anything to do with him. He worked his insides out to get through medical school, but he did really well. He did his physician's training and set himself up in city practice. Then he inherited Bindenalong. As well as being successful he was suddenly also rich—too rich, some would say. For a young man who'd come from nowhere, it was a lot to handle.'

'And he wasn't married then?'

'No. He met Sarah just after his inheritance came through—or rather she made sure she met him. His inheritance was in the papers, and all of a sudden he was socially desirable.'

'I see,' Rose said slowly.

'I don't know that you do,' Roy said bluntly. 'Ryan was young and overworked. He was also very much alone. He'd driven himself so darned hard there was no time along the way to get a social life. And Sarah. . . well, she'd turn any man's head.'

'Was she. . .was she beautiful?'

'Yep. Still is,' Roy said morosely. 'Sarah'll be beautiful till the day she dies. Ryan hardly had time to think before she was engaged and married to him. Then the fun started. She started spending Ryan's money like it was going out of fashion. She turned Bindenalong into a real social mecca. Ryan put in an airstrip and Queensland society came flocking. With Ryan's money and Sarah's beauty. . . Well!'

'So?' Rose shouldn't be asking. She shouldn't be listening, but she wasn't going to stop now.

'So they seemed happy enough at first,' Roy said. 'I think Ryan was so darned busy he didn't have time not to be. He thought there was a family obligation to keep the farm going but he wouldn't give up his medicine.

There were a couple of blazing rows, I remember. Sarah saw their role as landed gentry, and Ryan's work interfered with that. She kept at him to give up his medicine, but he wouldn't.'

'So he ran the property and his practice?'

'His medicine came first,' Roy told her. 'I was working the property and we could always see that. Sarah hated it—she saw his medicine as interfering with their social life. She liked him being a doctor— she just didn't like him practising medicine. Anyway, she settled down after a while. Mostly she stayed at Bindenalong during the week, entertaining guests— unless she wanted to go to Brisbane to shop. And then came the fire. . .'

'The fire. . .?'

'What I know of how the fire started is only hearsay,' Roy told her. 'I'd been injured and was down in Brisbane by that time. The station-hands used to come and see me when they could and they told me. . .' He hesitated, as though suddenly reluctant, but then made himself go on. 'Allan Vincent was the younger brother of a friend of Ryan's. Ryan had employed him just after the poddy-rustling—when I was off work. He was young, magnificently qualified, and full of enthusiasm. He was also good-looking and naïve. According to the boys, Sarah was patronising to him when Ryan was about, but when Ryan was away. . .'

Rose stirred uneasily on her chair. She was suddenly reluctant to hear more. There was more coming, though. . .

'There were only the three of them in the house when the fire started,' Roy continued gravely. 'The housekeeper, Sarah and Allan. There were two self-contained flats attached to the main house—one for the housekeeper and one for the manager. The rest of us slept in separate men's quarters.'

Roy hesitated. He looked over at Rose, took a deep breath and continued.

'It was a Thursday night and Ryan wasn't expected back. He came, though. There was a problem with his consulting-rooms—he was on the third floor and the lift had broken down so he'd cancelled his appointments for Friday. By then he had his pilot's licence and his own plane so flew himself home. He landed at midnight, just as the house went up in flames.'

'It burnt. . .?'

'It must have been burning for a bit before he got there, but the men were just rousing as he arrived.'

'What. . .what had happened?'

'No one knows for sure,' Roy said frankly. 'But Ada, the housekeeper, says Sarah had insisted Allan join her for dinner. A candlelit dinner, her ladyship decreed, and the dining-room was full of candles. Ada said Sarah was pressing wine on Allan and pressing heaven knows what else on to him besides, and Ada was uneasy about them. She has a high sense of moral right and wrong, our Ada, and a nose for trouble. Her nose was working overtime that night. She went to bed early and woke to the smell of smoke.'

'Smoke. . .'

Roy nodded. 'It was a weatherboard homestead a hundred years old and there was no stopping the fire. Ada got out to find Sarah in the garden, screaming that Allan was still inside. Next thing Ada knows, Ryan and the two stockmen appeared.

'So. . .' Rose hesitated. 'So Ryan tried to get Allan out?'

Roy grimaced. 'That's the horrid part,' he said grimly. 'The manager's wing was brick and the fire had hardly taken hold of it. When Ryan arrived, Sarah was still screaming that Allan was in the house. She was hysterical and useless. Ada. . .well, the housekeeper's asthmatic, and the smoke had taken her to near-collapse, but she managed to tell Ryan that Allan had been drinking and might not have woken. Ryan assumed Allan was in the manager's wing, so he and the men wasted ten minutes searching the smoke-filled manager's residence.'

'And no Allan?'

'And no Allan,' Roy said grimly. 'And I reckon you can guess the rest. By the time they came out, Ada, the housekeeper, had recovered a bit and started thinking. She told Ryan—and it took some courage, with her asthma making it almost impossible to breathe and Sarah screaming at her that she was a lying old. . . Well, she told Ryan maybe they should look for Allan in Sarah's bedroom. Only, the fire by now was out of control. Sarah's bedroom—the master bedroom—was alight.'

'But Ryan went in. . .'

'The men tried to stop him but Ryan shrugged them off and went, finding Allan exactly where Ada had guessed he might be. Somehow Ryan got him out. A girder came crashing down just as they reached the bedroom window. By that time the stockmen had hauled hoses round and managed to get the pair of them free, but when they saw the kid's burns they almost wished they hadn't.' Roy took a deep breath. 'If Sarah had said ten minutes before. . . But Sarah preferred to have Allan Vincent dead and Ryan risk his life than admit that. . .'

'Oh, Ryan,' Rose whispered.

'There's worse,' Roy said savagely. 'Ryan. . . Ryan lay in that damned hospital for weeks and thought about what had happened. Sarah didn't come near. I was doing rehabilitation in the same hospital and you just had to mention his name to get a stream of gossip about him. The nursing staff were horrified. Sarah was too weak to visit him, according to Sarah. The smoke had affected her. Finally Ryan wrote—said he knew she'd been bloody lonely and he wasn't holding anything against her. Said that Allan was young and terribly hurt, and he had need of her. Told Sarah he'd divorce her so she could support Allan—marry him

and look after him. For Pete's sake, Allan Vincent was
a kid. She'd seduced him and he should have something
out of the ruins. I shouldn't know this either, but Ryan
couldn't write with his burned hands so a nurse wrote
the letter and the whole hospital knew five minutes
later.'

'So?'

'So nothing. So Sarah refused point-blank to go near
Allan. She finally came in to see Ryan and I reckon the
entire nursing staff eavesdropped. She apologised for
being unfaithful. Not for nearly killing Allan, mind,
but for being unfaithful. Said she didn't want Allan
because she abhorred physical deformity, but the doctors had told her Ryan would recover without severe
scarring, so she'd stay married to him. And Ryan sat
up in bed and told her to get the hell out of his life and
never come back.'

Silence. Rose couldn't take it in.

'And it doesn't seem to have affected Sarah at all,'
Roy said drearily. 'Her lawyers demanded a divorce
settlement and Ryan paid it without a demur—I think
he just wanted to be shot of her. She's still playing
ladies among the social set here. Ryan, though. . .
Ryan's never been back to Bindenalong and I didn't
think he'd ever look at another woman. Until you. . .'

'Oh, Ryan,' Rose whispered. 'Oh, Ryan. . .'

'Now, you won't be telling him I've told you this,'
Roy said uneasily. He stood and took his glass over to
the sink. 'It's more than my job's worth.'

'Oh, Ryan. . .'

CHAPTER TEN

RYAN appeared two hours later.

Rose had showered and was in her cabin when she heard him arrive. She was trying to accustom herself to the sight of the new Rose—Rose in the Cinderella-at-the-ball dress. She heard a swift interchange between Ryan and his secretary, then sounds from the next cabin as Ryan showered and changed. Finally he emerged. She heard him pour himself a drink and a moment later there was a knock on her door.

'Ready?'

Rose opened the door. 'Yes,' she whispered.

The girl who emerged from Rose's cabin was stunning. The dress had worked its magic, and Rose's brilliant hair and her huge green eyes in her finely boned face gave her an air of almost translucent loveliness. Roy stood when she appeared and gave a low, stunned whistle. Then he looked uncertainly at his boss.

Ryan was holding a drink in one hand. He had been in the process of lifting his glass to his mouth but his hand now stayed motionless. So did his eyes. Where Roy's eyes lit with admiration, Ryan's froze to lose all expression. Carefully he put his drink down on the table.

'Shall we go then, Dr O'Meara?' he said, and his voice was grave and calm. It was as if he had rebuked her.

Rose took a deep breath and nodded. As her appearance had created an impression on Roy, so did Ryan's appearance on her. In the deep black of his dinner suit he looked impossibly handsome, and the look of him was enough to wrench at Rose's heartstrings. The story

Roy had told her had made him seem vulnerable, and yet he didn't look vulnerable now. He looked aloof and alone—a man who had need of no one, least of all her.

'I'm ready,' she said, a little unsteadily.

'I've ordered you a taxi,' Roy told Ryan. He smiled across at Rose, his eyes warmly reassuring. 'Off you go, Cinderella. Enjoy your ball.'

Rose flushed. The Cinderella comparison was not hers alone, then. She cast another look up at the man at her side, but Ryan's eyes were still repelling. She gave an involuntary shiver.

'The lady's cold, boss,' Roy said, his voice holding a hint of admonishment.

'I'm not,' Rose said quickly, and walked to the door. She had to get this over with fast. She looked back at Ryan's cold grey eyes. 'Please. . . Please—let's just go.'

The night was an interminable tangle of faces, talk, laughter—and questions! Every person Rose talked to was full of questions. Most of the doctors Rose had met that afternoon were present, and away from their role of examiners they were frankly delighted and intrigued by their new colleague. Once they arrived at the party, Ryan left Rose's side, as though relieved of an onerous social duty, and she was left to field questions as best she might.

Standing in the elegant, crowded rooms, Rose's overwhelming sensation was that of bereavement. She saw Ryan occasionally as he moved among the other guests but they might have been a world apart. Rose balanced her cocktail, answered another question, and felt as if part of her were dead.

What part? The part that loved Ryan Connell, she answered herself, and she knew it was true. It wasn't needed. Her heart had gone out to this solitary, aloof man who needed another woman as much as he needed more money. She looked bleakly across at him and then forced a smile as the people around her enjoyed a joke.

'So, you too want to bury yourself in Kora Bay?'

Rose swivelled around. When they had arrived Ryan had pointed out the chairman of the panel assessing the request for hospital registration. Now the chairman was approaching and smiling.

'I wouldn't call it burying,' Rose told him firmly. 'Kora Bay is the most beautiful town in Northern Queensland. It deserves its own hospital.'

'There's a good service at Batarra.'

'Yes,' Rose agreed. 'But it's two hours away by road. And sometimes that's just too far. . .' She took a deep breath. 'For instance, we've recently had to operate on board Dr Connell's boat. First we had a small girl with a strangulating hernia. . .'

And Rose told them of the successful operation on Cathy. Then she started talking of the loss of the baby just last week.

She was aware that the conversation around her had hushed. More people than the chairman were listening to her. Rose blocked out her nervousness as she told her harsh story, and the poignancy of the baby's death permeated the room.

Once, as she talked, Rose raised her eyes to Ryan. He was standing twenty feet from her, listening, it seemed, but as she looked up the man on his right made some comment. Ryan turned back to his companion and Rose's sense of desolation deepened. She had to force herself to keep going.

'Well, Dr O'Meara.' The chairman smiled as she finally finished. 'You present a convincing case. And the arguments Dr Connell gave us this afternoon were conclusive. The population can support a hospital and we're not the ones to stand in your way. We'll be there next week for inspection before registration.'

'That's wonderful, sir,' Rose said thankfully. She

looked across to see Ryan excusing himself from the group around him and coming towards her. The duty look was back in his eyes and she flinched.

'Does that mean we have our hospital?' Ryan asked smoothly as he reached them, and the chairman laughed.

'Was there ever a doubt?' He smiled. 'How much money have you sunk into the place? You wouldn't do that unless you were damned sure we'd agree.'

'I guess I wouldn't.' Ryan smiled.

'I must admit you had me wondering though, Ryan,' the chairman added. 'I couldn't see why in blazes a physician of your standing would end up in a place like Kora Bay.' His eyes went back to Rose and he smiled. 'And now I know.'

Rose flushed. His inference was obvious.

Ryan was smiling smoothly. 'As you say, sir.' He took Rose's arm. 'And now if you'll excuse us. . .'

'Certainly,' the chairman smiled, beaming his approval at two young lovers.

'I think we can go now,' Ryan said softly as they turned away, and Rose's eyes flew open with surprise. Was he feeling as eager to be out of there as she was?

'Unless you're enjoying yourself?' he added. Rose opened her mouth to reply and then stopped as a stir by the door caught her attention.

The woman who walked in was the most stunning creature Rose had ever seen. She was tall and impossibly slim, with smooth honey-blonde hair that hung to her waist in gleaming glory. Her skin was flawless, and what Rose saw most was skin. The woman's tiny gown was white silk, slashed low across her breast, clinging revealingly to her stunning figure and then slashed again to reveal elegant thighs and legs that were long and lovely. Her limpid blue eyes surveyed the room with amusement and a touch of condescension. She was on Ed Matherson's arm.

'Charles,' she drawled to the chairman. 'I guess you

medical fraternity have almost forgotten me, but Ed was. . .'

And then she caught sight of Ryan and her words died on her lips.

'R. . . Ryan,' she faltered. 'I thought. . .'

'You thought I wouldn't be here,' Ryan said drily. He flashed a hard look across at Ed. Ed's malicious enjoyment of the situation he'd so obviously engineered was obvious. 'As you see, Sarah, you were mistaken.' Ryan turned to face the woman directly, and his face turned to the light. The scar on his forehead made him seem harsh and forbidding. 'Does it offend you that I show myself in public—or do you think my scars are sufficiently faded?' He shook his head. 'Never mind, Sarah. I believe I was just leaving. Rose?' He turned back to Rose and held out his hand.

And for a second—no, not even for a second, for a fraction of an instant—Rose hesitated.

It was enough. The hand was withdrawn. 'As you wish,' Ryan said harshly. 'The car will be waiting when you're ready. Maybe you two should get to know each other. Rose, this is Sarah. Good evening.' And he was gone.

There was a deathly hush in the room. All eyes were suddenly on Rose, and Rose stood rooted to the spot.

Her anger rose to rescue her. For one crazy moment she wanted to run, to flee after the angry man who had just left. She had her pride, though, despite the trampling to which Ryan Connell had subjected it. So she stayed, and the Rose she didn't know—the Rose who fitted these damned clothes—rose to her aid.

'So you are Sarah,' she smiled, and held out her hand.

'Who the hell are you?' Sarah was flushed and angry and didn't care who saw it.

'I'm Ryan's new partner,' Rose said softly, watching the other girl's palpable anger. Rose flashed a swift, insincere smile at the obnoxious Ed. Around them was absolute silence. The room could fairly be said to be agog. 'And, as Ed can tell you, I'm also his friend.'

'Some friend,' Sarah sneered. 'If a man treated me like that I'd know what to do.'

'Maybe Ryan has reason,' Rose answered. She took a deep breath. 'Maybe you make him remember that he's scarred, betrayed and, by marrying you, partly responsible for the disfigurement of a fine young man.' She turned back to the chairman. 'If you'll excuse me,' she said simply, 'I think I should go too.'

'Of course, my dear,' the chairman said, and his eyes were suddenly warm. 'You go after him. This is the first time we've seen Ryan since the accident and we're all exceedingly pleased to have him back in the medical profession, even if it is in some damned out of the way place. If it's your influence. . .' he cast a flickering look of dislike across at Sarah '. . .if it's the influence of a caring woman that's making our Dr Connell human again, then we'll not stand in your way. Oh, and Dr O'Meara. . .'

'Yes?' Rose was slightly taken aback by the warmth she suddenly felt around her. Sarah was standing uncomfortably by the door, her eyes venemous. Somehow Rose had to find the courage to smile and walk straight past her.

'Good luck with your new hospital,' the chairman told her. 'And your new partner.'

As Ryan had promised, the car was waiting by the door as Rose emerged on to the darkening street. She shook her head as the driver swiftly moved to open the door for her.

'I'll walk,' she told him. She didn't know where Ryan had gone. She assumed he was doing the same as her, walking back to the boat.

Rose could leave now. There was nothing holding her to Brisbane any longer, and she didn't have to return to Kora Bay with Ryan. She could walk to the

bus station and board a bus and be home by tomorrow
night. She looked down at her beautiful dress and
grimaced. This was hardly the apparel for a twenty-
four-hour bus ride, but then what she wore was not
important. What people thought of her was not
important.

It wasn't quite true, she acknowledged to herself.
What Ryan Connell thought of her was important—so
important that she would go back to the boat. She
would try one last time to make him see that she was
no Sarah—that she and Sarah were so different that
they shouldn't be compared.

What was she saying? Rose walked slowly along the
still warm pavement, oblivious to curious looks or the
slowing of cars as they passed. She wasn't dressed for
a lone walk along Brisbane streets, but she didn't care.
Rose let her mind slowly come to terms with what she
had learned that day, and as she did, she realised that
things had changed.

This morning Rose had known that she loved Ryan
Connell and that that love was hopeless. She had called
herself Cinderella, and had thought that Ryan was so
far out of her league as not to consider her. Now. . .
Now she knew the agony a heartless woman had put
him through. 'I could show him what love really is,'
she whispered. If only she had a chance. . .'And I can't
gain that chance by getting on a bus back to Kora Bay,'
she told herself resolutely. 'I have to go back.' Uncon-
sciously her steps quickened as she made her way back
to the harbour.

The *Mandala* was in darkness when Rose reached it
and she grimaced. She'd forgotten Roy had taken the
night off. Rose walked forward to try the door, mentally resigning herself to a long wait on deck, but to her
surprise the door opened inward at her touch.

Ryan was seated by the bar with his back to the
door. He was in the dark, but the moonlight shining

through the windows was enough to show Rose his silhouette.

Rose didn't turn on the light. It seemed wrong somehow—an intrusion into personal pain.

'Ryan?' she said softly.

He turned, his drink jerking in his hand. As he saw her he swore, and put his drink down on to the bar with a bang. 'I didn't hear the car,' he said roughly.

'I walked.'

There was a long silence. Rose stood motionless, unsure how to approach this solitary man. He had never seemed so alone.

'I suppose I should say I'm sorry,' Ryan said at last. 'Walking out on you. . .'

'I understand.'

'Do you?' He laughed without humour. 'Go to bed, Rose.'

'Not. . . Not yet.'

The silence stretched on and on. Like the darkness, it was infinite.

And with the silence came the knowledge of what she must do. This man was past offering love. He had given it once and had it flung cruelly back at him. Maybe—just maybe—Rose had enough for both of them. She had her pride too, but this afternoon Rose's pride had been put aside with the realisation that it wasn't she who was hurt so deeply that part of her had died. Rose closed her eyes, searching for courage, and then opened them to walk slowly across to the bar. Ryan stayed where he was, with his back to her.

'I'll go,' she said gently. 'But Ryan, before I do, I want to thank you. You've given me so much. . .' She placed her hand on his shoulder and felt his body stiffen.

'It's nothing,' he said roughly, still not turning. 'I'm glad I was in a position to help.' His tone was so formal that Rose winced. He was pushing her away with a barrier so hard and cold that it was almost a physical presence between them.

'There's something else,' Rose whispered, and she cringed inside at what she was doing. She was wide open, exposed to raw pain that was threatening to overwhelm her. Her fingers lifted fractionally from Ryan's shoulder and then fell again to rest. 'Ryan, I want you to know that I love you. Regardless of the rights and wrongs, or of how stupid I'm being, I've fallen so far in love with you that you have my love for ever.' She closed her eyes. 'I want you to know that. I know you don't want my love—I know you can't return it—but my love is there. It's something I can't help. I love you, Ryan Connell, and I'll keep on loving you until the end of time.'

He stirred then, his shoulder shaking off her hand as if it burnt. In one swift movement he was off the stool and standing back to face her. 'You don't know what you're saying,' he said at last.

Rose gave a tiny, mirthless laugh that was almost a sob. 'No,' she said bitterly. 'I don't suppose I do. I sure as heck didn't want to say that, Ryan, but it seems to me that maybe you should know what. . .what's there for the taking. If only you want it. . .'

'If only I want it. . . If only I want you,' he said slowly.

'Yes.' Rose looked up at him, wanting to see the expression in his eyes but unable to in the dark. 'If you ever want me. . .'

'Don't Rose!' The words were flung at her like a blow and Rose put her hands up instinctively, as if to ward off impending pain. 'Don't you have any pride?' he demanded.

'No.' A tear slipped from Rose's brimming eyes and fell uselessly down her cheek. 'I don't. I lost my pride the first time I met you. It's gone. . .'

'Oh, for heaven's sake. . .' Ryan wheeled away and walked angrily to the other side of the cabin. Once

again he stood with his back to her, staring out through
the plate-glass windows to the harbour lights beyond.
'Rose, if you feel sorry for me. . .'

'Feel sorry for you!' Rose gave an indignant gasp.
'Why on earth would I feel sorry for you?'

'In case you hadn't noticed,' Ryan said harshly, 'I'm
hardly physically appealing.'

'Hardly. . .' Rose wiped her hand across her cheek
angrily and drew in her breath. 'Ryan Connell, if you
think your scar makes you repellent. . . When all I
have to do is look at you and go weak at the knees. . .'
She crossed to where he stood. Standing behind him
she put a hand up to reach around and touch the scar
running across his forehead. Once again she felt him
flinch at her touch but her hand was insistent. She was
fighting with everything she had.

She had one chance, she told herself. One chance. . .
She had no pride. Her fingers ran the full length of the
scar and she pressed her body up to touch his as she
did. 'Ryan, your scar is you,' she whispered. 'And I
love you. . .'

'Rose. . .' It was the groan of a man torn in two.
Ryan's body was absolutely immobile. 'Rose,
don't. . .'

'Why not?' Rose couldn't believe she was doing what
she was doing. It was as if she was compelled. Like a
wild animal fighting for its survival when cornered, so
now Rose was fighting for life itself. 'Don't you want
me?'

He turned then, and Rose was pushed back with the
movement. Her skirt flared out as she spun and she
would have fallen, but Ryan's hands came out and
grasped her shoulders hard. 'Want you. . .' His voice
was strangled—thick with passion. 'My God, Rose, do
you know how much I want you? But. . .'

'But what?' she flung at him. 'If you want me, then
what else matters? What else. . .?'

'You're not human,' he said savagely. 'You're a wild

and lovely thing, but deep down you'll be like all the rest. . .'

'Like Sarah. . .'

'Like Sarah.'

Rose stood staring up at him, her breath coming in shallow, fast gasps. She had fought with everything she had—and she had lost. That he could look at her and say that she was like Sarah. . .

She put her hands on Ryan's arms and pushed herself away. He released her. They stood staring at each other across the darkened room.

'If you think I'm like Sarah then there's nothing more to say,' she whispered bleakly.

Rose didn't wait for the dawn to leave for Kora Bay. The bus left at three a.m. Well before then she had risen and pulled on her shabby skirt and blouse. The beautiful clothes Ryan had bought her lay neatly folded in a pile on her bed. They had nothing to do with her and she didn't want them. Let Ryan do with them as he willed.

She gathered her belongings and quietly slipped through the darkened main cabin. The big doors opened silently as Rose turned down the handle.

Where was Ryan? Sleeping soundly in his cabin? Dreaming of who? Sarah? Or. . .? Or was Rose somewhere in his dreams?

She didn't care. She couldn't allow herself to care. From this moment, Rose O'Meara was back on her own. By the time Ryan arrived back in Kora Bay she would have her head down working. Somehow they would establish a professional relationship and go from there. Somehow. . .

CHAPTER ELEVEN

IT WAS two weeks before Ryan Connell returned to Kora Bay, and by the time he did Rose was wondering whether he intended to return at all.

The hospital was ready to operate. All Rose's fittings were in place. The nursing staff, self-conscious in their new uniforms, were eager for patients, and both Rose and the locum operating in Ryan's stead were eager to admit them.

'Do you reckon if he doesn't come back then there might be a job for me?' the locum asked. Ted Bryant was young and eager and had leaped at the locum position in Kora Bay in the hope that there might be a longer term position. Rose flinched.

'Dr Connell has to come back. He owns the hospital.'

'Owning the hospital doesn't mean he has to work here. There are plenty of absentee landlords. Now it's up and almost running I reckon he might make a tidy profit selling it.'

'Well, neither of us is in a position to buy,' Rose said brutally. 'So maybe we'd better hope he comes back.' She looked around her at the gleaming corridors just aching to be filled. 'The inspection team comes on Monday. He'll have to be back by then.'

'Not necessarily,' Ted said stubbornly, refusing to let his hopes die. 'I'm not applying for other jobs yet.'

It seemed Ted might be right. The inspection team arrived on Monday without any sign of Ryan.

'He's filled in all the necessary papers,' the team-leader told Rose. 'All you have to do is show us what's here.'

So Rose and Ted did the honours, leading the team

172

through. There was never a doubt as to the outcome. The newly appointed nurses were bristling with efficiency and eagerness to impress. All they wanted was patients.

And it seemed they could have them.

'You've done a fine job,' the team-leader told the two doctors, and Ted smiled with Rose.

'We intend to keep doing it,' he assured them, and Rose flinched. She liked Ted Bryant, but not. . .not if his presence meant Ryan stayed away.

And then the *Mandala* returned. It slipped into the harbour late one night. The next morning one of Rose's patients told her the news as she removed a foreign body from his eye.

'I guess he's just coming back to check up on you.' Her patient was a thin, wiry man in his fifties, who ran the local hotel. 'I don't expect he'll hang around now. He's got this place up and running and it'll be a nice little earner for him. Decent bloke, this Ted Bryant. Town's got two good doctors now.'

Rose managed a smile. 'There. It's out. You were lucky it didn't pierce the pupil. It'll feel as if there's something still there for a few days, but it's only the scratching that does that. I want these drops put in three times a day and I want you to buy some safety goggles on the way home. Wear them from now on when chopping the wood.'

'Yes, ma'am.'

Rose smiled her farewell but her heart wasn't in it. So Ryan was back. Why?

It seemed he was back to formalise his goodbyes. As Rose finished surgery that evening their new receptionist met her with the news. 'Dr Connell's waiting in the office,' she told Rose. 'With Dr Bryant. He wants to see you both.'

So he wouldn't even see her alone. Rose took a deep breath, dug her hands deep in her pockets of her white coat, and opened the door through to the office. She had to get this over with fast.

Ryan was staring out of the window to the ocean as she entered. Ted was seated behind the big desk, his face clearly puzzled. His expression lightened as Rose entered and Ryan turned.

Ryan was exhausted. Whatever he had been doing in the last two weeks, it hadn't been sleeping. Rose looked at the lines of strain etched on his face and longed to smooth them away. If only. . . She caught herself angrily.

'Welcome back,' she said stiffly.

Ryan's face was grim. 'Thank you,' he told her. 'Though, I'm not staying. I was just explaining to Ted that his job could be permanent if he wants it.'

'I want it,' Ted said eagerly. He looked uncertainly up at Rose. 'We can work together, can't we, Rose?'

'Of course,' Rose made herself say. Ted was competent and enthusiastic. She had nothing against him. It was just. . . It was just that he wasn't Ryan.

'What are you going to do now?' she heard herself say, and Ted glanced at her curiously. It was impossible to miss the pain in her voice.

'Much the same as I was doing before I arrived. Roy and I will take the *Mandala* further up the coast. We'll have to get the legal side of things here worked out. I assume a rental basis for the consulting-rooms would be appropriate. I'll leave you to work out your own partnership details.'

'Fine.'

Ted stood then. He looked from one to the other, sensing undercurrents he knew nothing about. 'We'll have to meet with lawyers and accountants,' he said tentatively, and Ryan nodded.

'I've organised a meeting tomorrow morning at nine with the local lawyer. If you can both be available.'

'I can be there.' Once more Ted looked from Rose to Ryan. 'I've a patient waiting,' he said uncertainly. 'I have to go.' He walked out, and neither Ryan nor Rose saw him go.

All Rose saw was Ryan. Running. The man was running from a pain he couldn't escape. From people.

'Coward,' she said softly.

Ryan shook his head. 'I'm sorry, Rose. I let myself get involved. For a short, crazy time I let you close.'

'And you won't do that again?'

'No.'

'Not ever?'

He turned away. 'No,' he said flatly.

'Mr Sullivan came to see me the other day,' Rose told him. 'The man whose baby died. He came to thank us for trying.' She took a deep breath. 'That's all you can do,' she whispered. 'Try.'

'And sometimes trying is useless,' Ryan said flatly. 'What did we achieve by trying? A dead baby.'

'So we never try again? What sort of crazy logic is that?'

'It's the only logic that makes any sense,' Ryan told her. 'Leave it now, Rose.'

'You mean, leave you?'

'Yes.'

So that was that. Her future mapped out. It was a future she had dreamed of—running a medical practice and hospital in her beloved Kora Bay—but there was no fulfilment of a dream in her heart as Rose went back to work. Only a leaden dreariness that wouldn't leave her.

They saw the lawyer at the appointed hour the next morning and the formalities were quickly finalised. Ryan's lease was amazingly generous, but when his lawyer demurred he shook his head.

'I've two fine young doctors here who can't afford a hefty rate,' he growled. 'I'd rather have enthusiasm running my hospital than money.'

Ted Bryant could hardly stop grinning. The only thing marring his enjoyment was Rose's quietness.

'It's a great thing for us, Rose,' he said firmly as they walked back into the hospital grounds. 'A chance like this. . . Well, I never dreamed it'd come my way.'

'Doctor!'

Ted paused and looked up. Their new charge sister had hurried out of the main doors and there was no mistaking the urgency in her voice.

'Thank heavens you're back. The lawyer said you'd already left. . .'

'Problem?'

'Mrs Carlyon came in half an hour ago. She's thirty-five weeks pregnant and came in because her ankles and fingers are practically puffing while you watch. I've measured her blood pressure and it's sky-high.'

Rose grimaced. May Carlyon. She knew her. The girl had been going to Batarra for ante-natal checks.

'How high?' she demanded, and when the sister told her she winced.

'We need a urine sample.'

'I already have it,' the sister told her as the three moved swiftly inside. 'Do you think. . .?'

'Is she by herself?'

'I was with her until now. She's in Casualty.'

Rose was already running. Pre-eclampsia. It sounded certain. And the first rule was not to leave the patient alone. A secondary rule was not to run in a hospital corridor, but rule one was paramount. If it was as acute and severe as it sounded then the woman could fit at any moment.

May Carlyon hadn't fitted when they reached her. She was lying on the examination table, her face a mixture of fear and doubt.

'I'm sorry to worry you, Rose,' she said as Rose burst in. 'I've been going to Steve Prost up in Batarra, but this happened so fast. My ankles weren't nearly so puffy when I went to bed last night. I woke up with the most awful headache and. . .and my eyes hurt so much with the light. . . So I got my husband to drop me here on the way to work.'

'You did the right thing,' Rose told her. She crossed to the switch and dimmed the light, then turned to the sister. 'The urine sample?' She hardly needed to test. The photophobia, headache and swelling were classic symptoms of eclampsia almost to the fitting stage.

'It's here.'

'I'll test it,' Ted said grimly. 'You check the baby.' He knew as well as Rose that everything depended on her examination. Thirty-five weeks. It might be OK. . .

The baby had lost none of its bounce. Rose checked its heart and was relieved to find nothing appeared wrong with the unborn infant. Despite its mother's illness, the baby was viable. Still, thirty-five weeks was early. She left May with the nurse and went to find Ted.

'Protein,' Ted said grimly. 'Lots of it. Hell, Rose, with that blood pressure she could fit any time. Plus photophobia. . .'

'I know.' Rose bit her lip. 'And it's happened fast.'

'Do we try and stabilise?'

It was every doctor's nightmare. Proceeding with the pregnancy was out of the question. This could turn into full-blown eclampsia at any moment, and the only way to stop it was to end the pregnancy.

The birth of the baby usually meant the condition worsened immediately after delivery. And if May was so ill already. . .

Ted shook his head. 'The blood pressure's too high. She'll fit for sure if we deliver now. But it's going to affect the baby pretty darned soon. The question is, how long do we wait? There's no way we can get it down enough to be out of trouble.'

'We'll send her up to Batarra.'

'No.'

'But Steve's her doctor. And they have a surgeon.'

'In two hours in an ambulance she could be dead.
You know that. We keep her quiet in a dark room,
administer hydrallazine and monitor the baby like a
hawk. As soon as the baby shows the least sign of
distress we deliver.'

'We deliver. . .' Rose thought back to the disaster a
few weeks ago. To deliver a premature baby with only
two doctors. . .

'We've trained nurses on hand,' Ted said solidly,
guessing her thoughts. 'And Rose—Ryan Connell's
still here. He'll help. The only reason I'd think of
sending her on to Batarra was if they had an obstetrician and paediatrician—or an anaesthetist who's
trained to do epidurals. They don't. We have a humidicrib and competent nursing staff. With three doctors
we can do this thing.' He hesitated. 'I've done a couple
of Caesars but. . . How's Ryan's skill?'

'He's good,' Rose said dubiously. 'But will he?'

'He will,' Ted said. 'If I have to go and drag him off
his fancy cruiser personally, he will.'

Two hours later they operated. May's blood pressure
had dropped, but as it did the child started to show
unmistakable signs of foetal distress. There was no
choice but to deliver.

So once again Rose performed anaesthesia while
Ryan Connell performed an emergency Caesarean.

He had come quickly when Ted called, striding
silently into the hospital and listening while Ted outlined his reasons for operating.

'I agree,' Ryan had said. 'We operate now.'

That was all. No argument. The decision was hardly
his to make. If Ryan refused to operate then they'd
lose the baby and May could die—and all of them
knew it.

It was so different this time. Instead of a white-faced
father standing in the background, waiting to try to
revive a lifeless baby, there were nurses, a humidicrib

and Ted Bryant. Rose administered the anaesthetic with care. She signalled Ryan as it took effect and he swiftly, skilfully made the incision.

The birth took moments. The child was waiting for him. Ryan's careful fingers scooped a tiny, perfectly formed baby girl into the world, and the whole theatre held its breath.

She had to be OK. The baby was hypoxic as a consequence of her mother's eclampsia—but surely they had reached her soon enough. She must. . . Rose was saying a tiny prayer over and over in her head. It mustn't be another tragedy.

Ted took the limp bundle from Ryan and bent over the tiny baby as Ryan went back to tending the wound. Swiftly Ted cleared the diminutive airways. Then he stood back and smiled in satisfaction as a thin, fretful wail broke the silence.

This baby, it seemed, intended to live. The wail strengthened as the little one voiced her displeasure at having been plucked from her comfortable cocoon. The outside world was obviously unsatisfactory from the newest Carlyon's point of view.

'I think she'll do,' Ted beamed happily. He looked over to where Ryan was closing. 'As long as her mother does.'

This was the dreadful time. The hours after the delivery were the most dangerous. Weak from anaesthesia, and still with high blood pressure, if May Carlyon was going to fit it would be now.

'I'll stay with her,' Rose said quietly. 'If you can take over everything else, Ted.'

'Sure.' Ted looked down with satisfaction at the bundle he was placing into the humidicrib. 'We could be on a winner here.' He turned to Ryan. 'Thank you for coming, Dr Connell,' he said softly. 'We were fortunate.'

Ryan nodded brusquely. He finished the dressing as Rose reversed the anaesthesia. 'We're not out of the woods yet.' He looked over to Rose. 'You won't leave her?'

'Not until her blood pressure comes down.'

'I'll be back at the boat if you need me.'

Rose nodded. She was concentrating on her dials. 'When. . .when are you leaving?' she asked.

'Tomorrow morning.' He turned to the sink.

'Ryan. . .'

'Yes?' He didn't look at her.

'We tried again,' she said softly. 'And we have a healthy baby. And if. . .if we're lucky, we'll have a healthy mother. A happy ending, Dr Connell.'

His eyes flew up and she met his look. Her eyes were straight and challenging.

'As you say, Dr O'Meara.'

He turned back to the sink.

Rose stayed in the ward all day, her eyes hardly leaving the woman in the bed. May Carlyon woke drowsily, saw her baby, smiled sleepily at her husband, whom they'd finally located cutting sugar, and then drifted back into an uneasy rest. Rose monitored her blood pressure and watched. Every hour that she stayed stable meant that she was closer to recovery.

And slowly May's blood pressure dropped. Not enough to lessen the guard, but enough to make Rose hope.

Ted dropped in during the day, and toward evening Rose looked up to find both he and Ryan approaching. She glanced up at Ryan and then quickly back to the bed. Ryan's face was non-committal—smoothly professional. It shouldn't matter in the least. It shouldn't.

'I think we might be winning,' she managed.

Ryan performed a swift examination and smiled down at the drowsy woman on the bed. 'I'm sure of it,' he agreed. 'Now, sleep, Mrs Carlyon. And lots of it. Your young daughter is running the nursing staff ragged already. This might be the last uninterrupted sleep you get for years.'

May Carlyon gave a sleepy, happy chuckle and drifted back into slumber.

'I've arranged one of the nurses to special Mrs Carlyon tonight,' Ryan said briefly. 'I'll be at the boat if you need me.'

'But. . .'

'There's no need for you to stay playing Florence Nightingale,' Ryan told her. 'Go home, Dr O'Meara. We're looking after this patient now.'

Rose nodded numbly, rose and left.

When she returned to the hospital the next morning Ted was at Mary's bedside. 'It's looking good,' he said briefly as Rose approached. 'Our esteemed physician has just done his rounds and pronounced himself satisfied. You've just missed him.'

'He's leaving?'

'Not until tomorrow.' Ted looked down. 'Though I think he might as well.' On the bed May stirred and opened her eyes. 'Good morning, Mrs Carlyon. Welcome to the morning. Your daughter's been asking for you.'

May smiled sleepily up at them. 'It seems like a dream,' she whispered. 'That we have a daughter.'

'A happy ending,' Ted beamed. 'That's what we like.' He looked up and waved as a young man with a worried look entered the ward. 'Here's the proud father. Been handing out cigars?'

'I haven't been game,' the young father confessed. 'Do you think. . .?'

'Now's the moment.' Ted signalled to the sister. 'Do we have any nice fat cigars in the drug cupboard?'

'Dr Bryant!' Sister scolded, then smiled. 'Will a cup of tea do?'

John Carlyon nodded gratefully. 'When. . .will I be able to take them home?'

Rose grinned. Things were a far cry from yesterday.

'Not for a week or so,' Ted said severely. 'The baby's still very small and your wife's blood pressure isn't normal yet. We'll hold on to them for a while before you take them home.' Then he looked up to Rose. 'But that's where you should be, Dr O'Meara. It's your day off. I'm on duty and it's a beautiful Saturday. Home!'

'Yes, sir.' Rose raised her eyes in mock-salute and left them. As she walked out of the hospital doors Ryan Connell emerged from the shadows to meet her.

'Dr O'Meara,' he said in satisfaction. He glanced at his watch. 'Punctual to a fault, I see.'

'Punctual. . .?' Rose frowned. 'I'm not. . .'

'Dr Bryant did tell you you had an appointment?' He frowned.

'But I don't. . .'

'Lunch,' he said, taking her arm. 'With me.'

Rose shook her head. 'Ryan, I'm not going anywhere with you,' she managed.

'Yes, you are,' Ryan said firmly.

'But. . .'

'No.' She was propelled firmly forward towards the waiting car. 'The word "but" has been my line. No more buts, my lovely Rose. Not now. Not ever.'

Ryan didn't speak again for thirty minutes. In that time he had driven to the marina, ushered her out of the car and on to the boat, and started the big cruiser's engine. Whenever Rose started to expostulate he shook his head and said nothing.

Rose sat numbly on deck as Ryan took the wheel and nosed his boat towards the reef. She was torn between dull despair and a crazy forlorn hope. She didn't look at the man at the wheel. She couldn't. She stared out to the wide blue ocean and her heart whispered the same crazy prayer over and over again. Please. . . Please. . .

Finally Ryan anchored, at a place where a band of coral cays formed a protective half-circle around the boat. The water was shallow and blue and gold, with sunlight dappling on the coral hidden beneath its surface.

Rose hardly saw. She was past registering her surroundings. Please, her heart was pleading. Please. . .

'Now,' Ryan said softly as he finished dropping anchor and came towards her. 'I thought I'd abduct my crocodile-hunter and have my own personal crocodile-hunt. A last adventure, if you like, before I leave this place.'

Before I leave this place. . .'You'll hardly find a crocodile out here,' Rose whispered desperately as he came closer. 'Ryan. . .'

'No crocodiles?' He sounded disappointed.

'No crocodiles. They hardly ever come out to sea.' This was a crazy conversation. Crazy!

'Then what shall we look for?' Ryan said soberly. He stooped to take her cold hands between his stronger ones. 'What does one look for on coral reefs?' He smiled as though he had just thought of something. 'I know. How about sunken treasure?'

'Ryan. . .'

'Come on,' he said strongly. 'A dive, Dr O'Meara. A treasure-hunt. . .'

Maybe a dive would be better than sitting here, Rose thought desperately. She pulled back her cold hands, avoiding Ryan's teasing grey eyes. Anything. . .

Last time they had dived together Rose had led Ryan. This time it was different. This time it was Ryan who was in charge, helping the white-faced girl into her diving suit, lowering her over the side, following her into the water, and then taking her hand and guiding her passive body through the wonderland of the coral garden below the boat.

The coral had lost its magic. For the first time in her life the dive did not shift Rose's heavy load of misery.

She didn't know what Ryan was doing to her. She only
knew that every time she saw him the pain was worse.
She let him lead her on, her rubber-clad body gliding
through the water with practised ease but her whole
being aware of just one thing—the linking of her hand
with his.

Suddenly Ryan's body jerked back, and Rose was
jolted out of her reverie. She peered forward through
the sunlit water to see why Ryan had stopped.

He had found something. Ryan's hand disentangled
itself from hers. Beckoning her to follow, he swam
downward to where a giant clam lay feeding on the
ocean floor. Ryan placed a hand underneath the huge
clam shell and then raised it in triumph. In it he held a
small, salt-encrusted box.

Rose stared at it in astonishment. She put a hand out
to touch it. The chest had been in the water for years
by the look of it. It was brass with rings at either end,
about the size of a shoe-box.

Ryan was holding his hand out imperiously for hers,
cradling the chest to his body with his other hand as he
signalled Rose to surface. Rose followed obediently.

Ryan semed excited by his find. It had distracted
Rose for a moment, but only for a moment. The misery
was returning. No treasure could take away the ache in
her heart.

Back on the boat Ryan stripped away his wetsuit and
then assisted Rose from hers. The chest lay between
them on the deck like a tantalising promise. Despite
her numbing confusion, Rose was interested.

'Open it,' Ryan told Rose. 'If you can.'

'You found it,' Rose said. She bent over the small
chest. 'It's your prerogative to open it.'

'No.' Ryan stood above her, clad only in his brief
bathing-costume, his tanned body dripping water on to
Rose. 'Sea-witches always have first choice of treasure
from the sea. Or. . .'

'Or what?' Rose said softly.

'Don't you know?' Ryan answered, kneeling down on the other side of the chest. 'Or they put a spell on those who refuse them their right. They bewitch them. Open it, my Rose.'

'I'm not. . .'

'Open it.'

Rose looked uncertainly up at him. Ryan's grey eyes were intent but they were on her, not on the small metal chest. Rose looked quickly away.

'It will be corroded shut—if it's not locked,' she faltered as she placed her hands on the lid. 'It should be opened by experts. . .'

She paused in amazement. The lid swung open, as if it had been oiled yesterday, to reveal what lay inside.

The salt-encrusted chest contained one thing and one thing only. An exquisite diamond ring lay in lonely splendour on a bed of crimson velvet, twinkling up at Rose as the sunlight caught its brilliant surface.

Rose's breath drew in on a gasp. This was no treasure from years gone by. The ring looked as if it had been placed there yesterday. . .

Yesterday. Rose's eyes flew to the man kneeling beside her, and once more his eyes were on her—not on this 'treasure'. His look answered her unspoken question.

'You planted this,' she whispered accusingly—wonderingly And she was aware that she had started to shake again. 'This is no sunken treasure, Ryan Connell. You placed it here.'

'A hard task it was too,' Ryan agreed gravely. 'And not without risks. I gave Roy a couple of days off and I couldn't dive by myself. The fishermen who brought me out this morning thought I was mad.'

'But. . . But why?'

'Because I married Sarah as a mortal,' Ryan said softly. He picked up the magnificent ring and placed it on her unresisting finger. The ring slid home as if it was meant to be there. 'I got it wrong, my Rose. I was treating you as someone who wasn't special and, Rose, you are the most special woman I could ever imagine. I've never known a woman like you. I bought you expensive clothes, Rose, and you left them without a backward glance, going back to your oil-stained shorts and your beloved medicine. You don't fit the women I know. . .the women I knew. I came back to Kora Bay to say goodbye and you gave me my miracle. You gave me courage to try again—to live again. So now I have the courage to tell you I love you, my sea-witch. I loved you from the moment I set eyes on you. You've bewitched me and you won't—you can't release me.'

He held her beringed hand in his and stared down at it, his mouth twisting in a wry grimace. 'So I'm asking, my love. I'm down on one knee, my sweetest Rose, and I'm asking. . .pleading with you to marry me.'

'But. . .' Rose could hardly find her voice. Tears were slipping down her cheeks unnoticed and the magnificent diamond was a brilliant blur in Ryan's grasp.

'No buts,' Ryan said quickly. 'Not now.'

Rose swallowed hard, searching for words. None came.

'I did some hard thinking this morning,' Ryan told her. 'I'd like us to stay here. Ted Bryant is breaking his neck to stay—and if he did then Kora Bay would have a medical team of three. That means we'd have some free time. You'd have your beloved Kora Bay and your medicine. With three doctors here you'd even have time for some crocodile-hunting on the side. And I. . . I would have you. What do you say, my Rose?'

She wouldn't let herself believe. Not yet. . .

'You made love to me before,' she whispered. 'In this place. And in the morning. . . In the morning it was over. Finished. You remembered that you couldn't trust.'

There was a long silence. A sea-bird swept low over the water, wheeled up as if the boat was interfering with its flight plan, and then swept down low again. Its wings touched the water, and the sea mirrored its fleeting image.

'It's true,' Ryan said at last. His hands took hers in his, and Rose's were cold to touch. He pulled her up to stand before him, her breasts resting lightly on his chest.

Rose's heart was so still she was scarcely breathing. The world, it seemed, was waiting. 'It's true,' he said again. 'And my mistrust nearly lost me the only thing that can make me whole again. My beloved Rose. . .'

Rose lifted her face to his. Her eyes were still troubled. This man of shadows. . .

'Do you know how much I hated Bindenalong after the fire?' Ryan asked. 'You can't guess. It represented failure and betrayal and near-murder. And yet, for me, Bindenalong was my past. It represented my only link with my family—a family I hardly knew—and when it first became mine I loved it. But it was a shadow. I went there last week,' he continued. 'I had to organise a new manager's residence for Allan. I walked around the place and the shadows threatened to overwhelm me.'

'So sell it,' Rose whispered, and Ryan shook his head.

'I never could,' he told her. 'Last week I knew I could never sell it, but I thought I could never live there.' His grip on her hands tightened. 'But now. . . How do you feel about building another house on the property? Our house. Our home, where the shadows mingle peacefully with our love. Where we can go for holidays when we've established Kora Bay as a vibrant, busy medical community. Where we can teach our children to love Bindenalong as well as Kora Bay. Where we and our children can let our shadows merge with love.'

'Oh, Ryan. . .'

'I'd never ask you to give up Kora Bay,' he said

anxiously. 'I know how much it means to you. You and your darned crocodile-hunting. . .'

Rose looked up to Ryan's anxious face and smiled tremulously through her tears. Her prayers were being answered, it seemed, and answered a thousand-fold. She lifted Ryan's scarred hand and laid it across her cheek. 'You know I can't find crocodiles alone,' she said tremulously. 'I keep thinking they're logs.'

'That's why you should marry me,' Ryan said firmly, the beginnings of a smile in his voice. 'My Rose, this is not a love that lasts until the morning. I know that now. I was crazy—crazy—not to see it before. This love. . . This love is for now and for the rest of our lives. I swear it to you. I swear that I'll spend the rest of my life finding crocodiles for my doctor, my hunter, my love. Or polar bears. Or elephants, if you ask it of me. Rose. . . Rose, you must marry me. I'm going crazy, my sea-witch.' He touched her face lightly with his finger. 'Rose, you are the most wonderful woman I have ever met, and I can't live without you. Please. . . Say you'll marry me.'

Rose could no longer see her love. Her eyes were blinded by tears. Her heart had started beating again, steadily, strongly, and each beat told her that she was loved. Now and forever.

'I'll marry you, my Ryan,' Rose whispered. 'Oh, my love, of course I'll marry you. My heart. . .'

"All it takes is one letter to trigger a romance"

Sealed with a Kiss—don't miss this exciting new mini-series every month.

All the stories involve a relationship which develops as a result of a letter being written—we know you'll love these new heart-warming romances.

And to make them easier to identify, all the covers in this series are a passionate pink!

Available now   **Price: £1.99**

MILLS & BOON

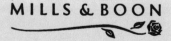

SLOW BURN
Heather Graham Pozzessere

Faced with the brutal murder of her
husband, Spencer Huntington demands
answers from the one man who should have
them—David Delgado—ex-cop, her
husband's former partner and best
friend...and her former lover.

Bound by a reluctant partnership, Spencer
and David find their loyalties tested by
desires they can't deny. Their search for the
truth takes them from the glittering world of
Miami high society to the dark and
dangerous underbelly of the city—while
around them swirl the tortured secrets and
desperate schemes of a killer driven to
commit his final act of violence.

"Suspenseful...Sensual...Captivating..."

Romantic Times (USA)

MIRA

Temptation

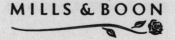

'Right Man...Wrong time'

All women are haunted by a lost love—a disastrous first romance, a brief affair, a marriage that failed.

A second chance with him...could change everything.

Lost Loves, a powerful, sizzling mini-series from Temptation continues in May 1995 with...

**What Might Have Been
by Glenda Sanders**

MILLS & BOON

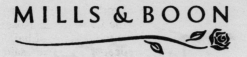

MILLS & BOON

LOVE ON CALL

The books for enjoyment this month are:

PRACTICE MAKES MARRIAGE	Marion Lennox
LOVING REMEDY	Joanna Neil
CRISIS POINT	Grace Read
A SUBTLE MAGIC	Meredith Webber

Treats in store!

Watch next month for the following absorbing stories:

TAKEN FOR GRANTED	Caroline Anderson
HELL ON WHEELS	Josie Metcalfe
LAURA'S NURSE	Elisabeth Scott
VET IN DEMAND	Carol Wood